◊◊◊◊◊◊◊◊◊◊◊◊◊◊◊◊

For *my best friend and wife, Pam, who's love, and encouragement helps me follow my passion.*

For *my sons, daughters, and grandchildren, always pursue your dreams.*

For *Key Yessaad, a brilliant coach, mentor, and friend, who envisioned the finish line, told me to get to work and stuck with me for the journey.*

◊◊◊◊◊◊◊◊◊◊◊◊◊◊◊◊

FROZEN HARVEST

JOSEPH BENEDICT

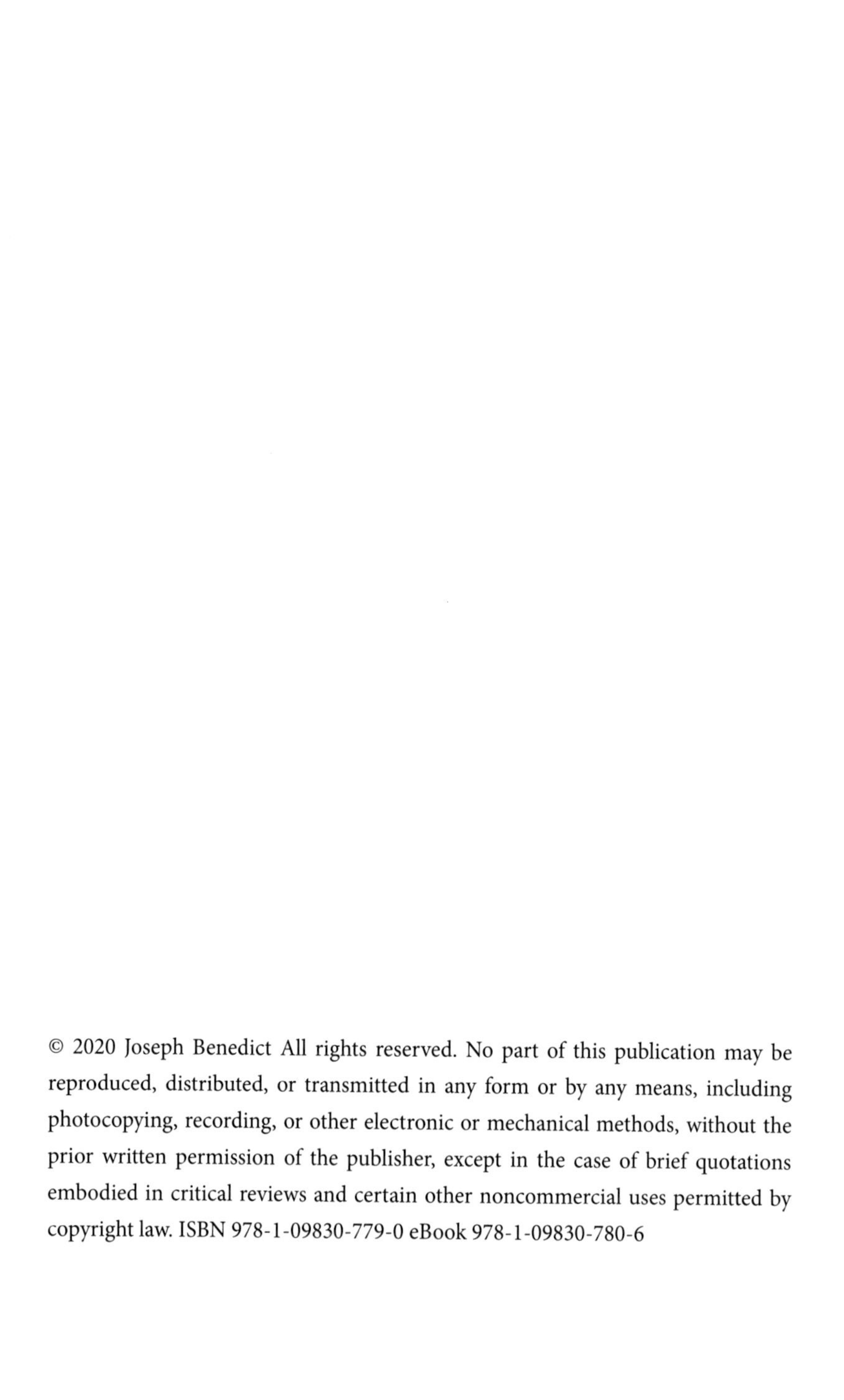

 ISBN 978-1-09830-779-0 eBook 978-1-09830-780-6

A blizzard is a force of nature with many facets that a mere observer would not comprehend from afar. However, a person immersed within the storm experiences its layers and nuances assaulting their senses with isolation, fury, and bone-chilling cold.

CHAPTER 1

(Present)

The weak winter sun could barely penetrate the grimy warehouse windows that lined the front of Joel Vicks' office. A lot of old warehouses in downtown Minneapolis had recently been converted into posh living quarters for up and coming thirty-something executives. Joel doubted the renovation craze would ever reach this particular building, though. The building was ugly and had no redeeming qualities as far as he could tell.

The concrete floor had dark stains and a faint smell of axle grease mixed with dirt. Someone once told Joel the building was formerly a carriage repair depot in the late 1800s. A heavy metal door, which slid on rollers, separated Joel's' office from the street where a small white sign with simple block letters, mounted too high for anybody to read, said, "J.V. DETECTIVE AGENCY."

It was the middle of December, and the snow plowed against the curb and sidewalk was nearly black from the exhaust and dirt-spattered by passing cars. When fresh snow blanketed the city, the existing piles transformed into what looked like miniature snow-capped mountain ranges. Within a couple of days, the dirt and grime reclaimed them, and the cycle started anew.

Joel, a tall man in his mid-fifties, leaned back in his vintage wooden swivel chair, staring into space, his feet propped up on a half-open drawer of his metal desk. The desk looked like it had come out of a government office, the battleship gray paint and boring design were consistent with Government Issue.

Joel's height and thick black hair had been a gift from his Grandfather on his Mother's side. His only memories of the man were his marathon coughing spells brought on by a lifetime of smoking hand-rolled cigarettes.

In the last couple of months, Joel's business had been slow. His most recent case involved a suspected cheating wife who met her lover in an adult book store near downtown on Wednesday around noon. The couple would climb into the back seat of the man's SUV after exiting the store. The SUV had heavily tinted side and rear windows and parked on the busy street in front of the store. The tinted windows and busy street presented a bit of a challenge for Joel in getting irrefutable proof of her suspected cheating.

After witnessing the couple's behavior on the previous Wednesday, Joel parked a nondescript rented van on the opposite corner of the block. The day was bright and brutally cold, and people who were out walked with purpose.

When Joel spotted the SUV slowing to park, he swung the rental van into traffic, and traveling the length of the block, pulled into space directly in front of the SUV. Joel pretended to look at his phone as he watched the driver through his side-view mirror. He waited until the man entered the store before moving to the back of the van, where his camera equipment was lying in protective cases on rubber floor mats. Joel slid a portable pull-up shade out of its case and set it up between himself and the front of the van. The shade prevented him from being backlit, and he now had a clear view through the windshield of the SUV.

One hour later, he had the incriminating pictures he needed for his client. The woman, a petite blonde who arrived smartly dressed in business attire, in his photos, was only wearing knee-high stockings. If it were not for the tragic fact that a family was about to be ripped apart, he would have considered the afternoon a success.

Joel's idle thoughts were interrupted by the low rumble of a mail jeep in the distance. It was a distinct sound, short accelerations between squeaking brakes. Nobody in their right mind would drive like a mail carrier, he thought. A minute later, he heard the metal scrape of his mail slot, followed by the splat of mail hitting the concrete floor.

An excuse to get some exercise, he smiled. He thought he might start going to the gym and try to lose the extra weight hanging around his waist like an unwanted visitor.

The mail, for someone self-employed, can be rewarding or depressing. There were several junk pieces and one letter style envelope which looked old and discolored. Joel stooped down and only picked up the letter.

The envelope had the soft texture paper gets when handled a lot. The cursive handwriting on the front had small ink blotches at the end of some words, leading Joel to surmised an old-style fountain pen was the instrument used.

The envelope had two stamps, one tired and aged, like the envelope and one crisp and modern looking.

Joel sat back down at his desk and turned the letter over in his hands several times. There was a small crease tear in one corner of the envelope. But for Joel, the return address of "Seven Lakes, Minnesota" was the most intriguing thing about the letter. He knew the place well, his family had vacationed there during the summers of his youth, and he had fond memories of the area.

Joel located a small knife in the top drawer of his desk and slit the envelope open along its top. The folded piece of unlined paper was double spaced and typed on an old typewriter that appeared to be out of alignment, judging by the spacing of the letters.

Dear Mr. Vick,

I read about your recent rescue of the little girl in Minneapolis.

Joel re-read the sentence, the rescue the author referred to had taken place at least ten years prior.

I have been haunted for years by visions of something I witnessed as a child.

I am the last remaining person alive who knows the truth about the disappearance of Mary Benton. I hope you will consider looking into the matter; she is a restless soul. I am not well, and time is of the essence.

Sincerely,
Timothy Williams

Joel leaning back in his chair, looked up at the peeling paint on the tin ceiling panels. The person who wrote this is probably dead, he thought. Unless Mr. Williams put something in writing, Mary Benton may have a hard time getting her story told.

Joel re-read the letter and found the statement about her being a restless soul interesting. Picking the envelope back up, he studied the return address. Seven Lakes County Health Center.

Joel googled it on his phone and realized it was a place he had seen before as a child. Today, it was no longer politically correct to call such facilities insane asylums or mental institutions, but the Seven Lakes Health Center is the former Lake Country Asylum. He remembered his dad driving by its iron front gates and in a shrill voice saying the crazy people are going to get you. As a child, Joel did not have a concept of a crazy person but remembered the looks of the place creeped him out. From the online description, the Center now appeared to be a Nursing Home run by the State.

Finding anything on Google about Mary Benton was proving to be a more difficult task. Joel spent over two hours searching phrases before finding a thin thread that led him to a short digitally archived newspaper article published in a town about forty miles north of Seven Lakes.

The date on the article was December 24, 1925. It read, "*Mary Benton, origins unknown, who is traveling alone, arrived in Seven Lakes by train on or around December 5 and had taken up lodgings at the Seven Lakes Grand Hotel. On the morning of December 23, she failed to return to her hotel room after venturing out into near blizzard conditions in the early evening hours of December 22. Local authorities fear she may have become disoriented in the storm, and likely died of exposure.*

Joel shook his head, "so I am guessing the spring thaw came and went, and she never turned up." He said to himself.

There was something attractive about the idea of leaving the cities behind and looking into this unusual request. Unfortunately, there did not seem to be a client who was hiring him, which meant he would not get paid.

Joel looked at the small puddles that had formed on the concrete floor from melted snow under his red 59 Bel Air.

He thought about what he would need for a couple of night's stay in Seven Lakes. He figured it would take at least that long to establish whether there was anything left to investigate in such an old cold case.

Joel called the Seven Lakes County Health Center and was encouraged when told they were unable to give out information about Mr. Williams, which meant he was probably still alive. Joel knew the only way to get this story was to visit Seven Lakes in-person.

CHAPTER 2

(Present)

When Joel started his career in the field of detective work, he quickly earned a reputation for solving cases where others had failed, notably missing person cases. He had a knack for assessing character and listened carefully to what people said before starting to peel back the layers to uncover the real story.

It was not about what a person said, but what they were not saying that he found informative. His logical mind and calm demeanor were assets he used to his advantage during investigative interviews.

The case that the strange letter referred to was the first time he had received any notoriety from his work. He had not paid much attention to the stories at the time; the successful conclusion of the case was enough of a reward. He knew that papers across the state had picked up the story and was pretty sure Williams must have seen an article before writing his letter.

The case had been a gut-wrenching affair, quickly capturing the attention of all the law enforcement agencies within the cities. A four-year-old girl vanished into thin air from her middle-class neighborhood home in Minneapolis. The investigation that ensued was swift and encompassed a massive commitment of resources. The picture the girl's family provided the media was the type that would rip your heart out.

For 24 hours, law-enforcement threw everything they had at the case and came up empty. They canvassed the girl's neighborhood exhaustively, and nobody had seen a thing. It was in the middle of the afternoon on July 2nd, when she went missing and people were preparing for the 4th of July holiday. She had been riding her bike with training wheels, and the bike left in the middle of the sidewalk faced straight ahead. One of the detectives who was first on the scene commented that it looked like the bike was carefully parked.

Two-story homes lined both sides of the residential avenue, and there were at least twelve nearby houses with a view of where the bike was left. A betting person would have liked the odds of someone seeing something. There was a small grocery store two blocks beyond the girl's home that usually added foot traffic along the avenue, but that angle also came up empty. The police conducted a house to house search in the immediate vicinity, and the compulsory interviews with family members revealed nothing suspicious.

Somebody with authority decided that it must have been a "stranger abduction" and the focus of the investigation shifted from the immediate neighborhood to a wider net. Still, with nothing to go on, it was not a promising development. The community which had been crawling with police one day earlier was now virtually empty of officers except for an occasional patrol car drive-by.

Joel called his friend Marty, who injured in the line of duty, worked a desk at the downtown headquarters. Marty explained there had been a shift in focus, and after spending hundreds of man-hours in the neighborhood, they had nothing to go on. When Joel saw a picture of the girl on the news, he decided to take a look at the site for himself.

There was still a piece of yellow crime tape wrapped around a maple tree on the boulevard when he drove down the quiet street. Other than that, there was no sign of the previous police activity or anything else out of the ordinary. Joel understood the clock was ticking, and every hour that passed decreased the chances of a successful resolution.

Stepping out of his car, he crossed the grassy boulevard and stepped onto the sidewalk near the tree with the crime tape. Standing in the middle of the pavement, he looked up and down the street at the houses that had a view of this spot. Marty had given him the address of the girl's house, and he saw those numbers above the door of a house sitting on top of a steep hill. There was a staircase that neatly split the yard in half with approximately 20 steps leading from the sidewalk to a landing and another set of five steps to the front door.

Joel looked up at the house for a few seconds before shifting his gaze to the grassy hill with its steep pitch leading into the side yard between the missing girl's house and the next-door neighbors'. Both houses were at the same elevation. Beads of sweat formed on his brow in the heat of the July afternoon. There were lush plantings and inviting shade between the homes, and just slightly back from the crest of the hill, a small kitten stalked an unseen prey under a lilac bush.

Looking back at the sidewalk where the bike would have been, he asked himself, how long it would have taken her to scramble up the hill? A few seconds? He saw that once she reached the side yard, she became invisible to just about everyone.

Joel was well-liked by local law enforcement because he had been one of them, and now that he was an independent investigator, he respected their jurisdiction and shared any information he had. He did not see the point of adversarial relationships that did not benefit either party. He knew there was an extreme focus on this case and understood there was nothing that got under the skin of police officers more than cases involving children.

Joel figured massive data searches were underway that would try to match the location and crime to possible suspects. Information was also shared nationally, and open cases compared to the details of this one.

Marty indicated that one of their best interviewers, Jack Hannigan, had talked with the family, and unequivocally said there was nothing there. Nobody had seen a thing on a summer day when a lot of people were off work and preparing for the 4th of July holiday. It didn't add up. It was dawning on Joel, that the lack of evidence, might be the best evidence that she had not been abducted at all and was still somewhere in the vicinity.

The more he looked at the scene, the more he was convinced she was still here. Something had probably caught her attention, and she carefully parked her bike in the middle of the sidewalk and scrambled up the hill to see what it was. When she did, she effectively disappeared from view. But where was she now?

Joel had driven around the block before parking on the street and noticed there were no alleys on this particular block. The lot sizes in his estimation were an acre or more. The elevation of the land dropped considerably from one end of the block to the other until leveling out on the far end. The missing girl's home was the third house in from the corner on the high side of the block. The backyards were extensive, and it appeared homeowners carved out the amount of area they wanted to maintain and let mother-nature tend to the rest. The natural areas, beyond groomed lawns, would be ideal places for forts and hide-outs.

He called Marty, and when he answered said, "she is here somewhere, I have a strong gut feeling she is still here."

Marty recognizing Joel's voice, said, "what do you mean?"

"I mean, I don't think she is gone, I am here on site, and it doesn't add up, she is still here somewhere," he said with conviction.

“Ok,’ Marty said, “take it easy, I will make a few calls” and hung up. Ten minutes later, Marty called back and asked Joel what he needed.

“I need help to conduct another search,” Joel said flatly.

Ten minutes later two squad cars pulled up in front of where Joel was standing, one officer jumped out, nodded at Joel, and climbed the steps to knock on the door of the missing girl’s home. The officer is explaining to a distraught father that they wanted to conduct another search behind the houses. Joel joined the remaining officers, and they climbed the steps together before walking between the houses into the backyard. He explained where he wanted the officers to concentrate their efforts and for them to pay close attention to any possible underground forts or hide-outs where she may have fallen.

An officer named Pete Stanley asked Joel why he was so sure she was here. Joel hesitated a couple of seconds and said: “because of the evidence.”

“What evidence?” Stanley asked.

“It’s all wrong,” Joel replied.

“The fact that nobody saw a thing in broad daylight when most people were home. Nobody saw a strange vehicle; nobody heard a sound; there is no sign of anything out of the ordinary; it doesn’t add up.”

The group made their way into the far reaches of the backyard and the overgrown areas between the girl’s home and its backyard neighbor.

About 20 minutes into the search, Officer Stanley called out that he had found something. Joel and the other officers converged on the area where Stanley held up a small tennis shoe dangling from the end of a stick. Joel knew it was the girl’s from the description her mother had given the media. The shoe was good news, she had been back here, and more than likely still was. The search party continued with a renewed urgency.

The news of finding the shoe was radioed back to headquarters and set things in motion that would soon bring dozens of additional officers to the scene.

The ground was soggy in the area where Joel searched, and he noticed and an unusual humped up protrusion running for several feet before disappearing into the denser brush. When he stepped on it, he found it to be hard under the dirt and weeds. Scraping at the earth with his foot, he uncovered what looked like an old drainage pipe.

Joel followed the pipe into the brush and saw that a portion of it was exposed, and there was a jagged hole in its surface, partially hidden under a bush. Joel knelt by the opening and estimated it to be about 18 inches wide by 12 inches tall. He called out for someone to bring him a flashlight. The urgency in his voice brought the other officers to his location. Grabbing the light from one of the officers, he stuck his arm and head into the hole and shined the light in both directions. He didn't see anything other than dirt, sand, and some vines that had breached the pipe through small cracks in search of water. When he shined the light straight down from the opening, he saw the dirt had been recently disturbed.

Holy crap, Joel said under his breath, she must have gone in, and couldn't get back out. The diameter of the pipe appeared to be tall enough for a small child to walk in an upright position. Joel could tell by the commotion around him that the Calvary was beginning to arrive. He pulled his head out of the opening and motioned for the closest officer. "I think she may have gone in there," Joel said, "We need to make a larger entry."

The officer talking into his radio, relayed the information to his captain who just arrived on site. The captain put out an order for a fire rescue truck with cutting equipment to enlarge the opening in the pipe. Within minutes a fire truck was dispatched from the neighborhood station. Several firefighters arrived within ten minutes carrying the requested cutting equipment and threaded their way between the houses to where the group of officers and residents had gathered.

The men made quick work of enlarging the opening and two crew members equipped with flashlights and radios dropped into the pipe and started crawling in opposite directions. Joel staying close could hear the rescuer's movements as they made their way down the inside of the pipeline. After several minutes the sounds from within the pipe faded, and he could only hear the intermittent chatter of the group around him.

Somewhere to his left, the radio came to life, "I have her, she's ok, she's ok." The simple sentence came through loud and clear, and a spontaneous cheer went up among the officers and residents, with several people high fiving and slapping each other on the back. Joel knew from his time on the force that successful resolutions were not the typical outcome, and he was thankful today, the good guys had won one.

CHAPTER 3

(December 5, 1925.)

Mary Benton had chosen Seven Lakes, Minnesota, as her destination because of an advertisement poster she had seen as a child. The sign hung on the walls of hundreds of train stations she traveled through with her mother. There was something about the subject matter that had conveyed to Mary, a sense of calmness and serenity that she never forgot.

The picture on the poster showed a clear blue lake with a wooden dock extending out from its shoreline — the scene inviting the viewer to be near the water. The reflection on the water from the setting sun, nearly aligning with the end of the dock, looked like a pathway straight to the horizon.

The title text across the top read: "Let our Pure Spring Waters Rejuvenate your Soul," and on the bottom, printed in tall narrow letters, "Seven Lakes Minnesota."

The scene and words spoke of things Mary had rarely experienced in her life. She was anxious most of the time and unable to relax fully. She dreamed of healing waters washing over her on a warm summer's day.

Every mile of track, Mary traveled created distance between her past and her new life.

She felt nervous when she boarded the train in Fairview and reaching over; opened her small suitcase. She heard the conductor on the platform calling for final boarding as she pulled out a worn piece of paper and gently unfolded it in her lap. The deeply creased paper was an advertisement she had carefully saved from a magazine.

The title across the top of the ad was identical to the train station posters, and it had the same tall letters at the bottom. The image on this ad, however, was different and featured a young woman smiling while riding her bike along a path that followed a lake's shoreline. The woman's legs stretched forward, her bare feet off the pedals as she coasted down an incline.

Mary studied the picture for several minutes, paying particular attention to the woman's expression before carefully folding it back up and placing it into her suitcase.

She heard the steam whistle forward in the distance and felt a slight lurch, a pause, and then another pull as the train began to move. Looking out her window, she watched the station's roof supports moving past, each one moving faster until the train cleared the platform, and sunlight flooded the car.

Mary remembered times when her anxiousness subsided because of the hospitality of a sympathetic family. Every so often, they received an offer of temporary lodging. The reprieve from the road had an opposite effect on her mother, though, and Mary could see her become restless after a few days.

It was during one of these stays that Mary experienced one of her most cherished memories. They had finished eating dinner with their hosts, and Mary and her mother retiring to the backyard were sitting together on a wooden bench swing. It was the golden hour of the evening where light obtains an exceptional softness and warmth, and her mother looking across at her had the most beautiful smile she had ever seen. Mary could always remember the intense feeling of contentment she felt at that moment and replayed the scene when she became scared or unsure of her future.

Since the Fairview Station was near the edge of town, it took only a few minutes for the train to leave it behind and roll into the open countryside.

It was a sunny day that belied an outside temperature well below freezing. The steam radiators designed to heat the passenger cars, and fed by the locomotive, did not seem to be working right, and Mary could feel a chill in the car, especially down low where the colder air pooled around her legs and feet.

Every possession she owned was in her two suitcases; her small bag in the seat next to her, and a more substantial matching one loaded into the luggage car in Fairview. Mary would arrive in Seven Lakes with her belongings and $73.00. The money had taken two long years to save, and despite the odds, she felt hopeful about her new life.

Seven Lakes, in her imagination, had always been warm with calm blue waters under cloudless skies. It was an unfortunate bit of timing that had her arriving in the middle of winter. She had never been in control of such details and always forced to adapt to situations the best she could.

As the train gathered speed, she felt the temperature in the car continue to drop, and looking around; she spotted a blanket in an unoccupied seat across the center aisle. The blanket slung across the back of the chair, had "Property of Northern Rail Company" stenciled near one border. Retrieving the cover, she wrapped it around her legs before sitting back down and holding the ends together in her lap. She had not realized how tired she was, and her drowsiness began replacing her anxiety. Today was her second full day traveling the rails, and the stress of venturing toward the unknown had taken its toll.

The side to side motion of the car had a relaxing effect, and she turned in her seat toward the window. Leaning against the seat-back, she watched the flat farmland interspersed with small patches of trees move across her view like a movie screen playing a feature film about the vastness of the north.

The light inside the car began to fade, and the only thing she could see now was a thin line of illumination underneath a door. She was awake, lying under covers, curled up on her side facing the door. She stared at the sliver of light until it blurred and became animated, expanding, and contracting in sync with her breathing.

She could not hear anything behind the door but felt tense and remained motionless as she continued to stare at the light and listened for signs of movement. Time was fluid and unmeasurable, and the light changed into a star and diamond pattern, similar to sunlight reflecting off the surface of a lake.

She now felt herself floating on the surface of the water as small swells moved her gently from side to side — the sun warm against her face and arms. Her head laid back, her ears partially submerged, caused sounds to be muffled and distant.

She saw herself from above, thousands of flashing reflections surrounding her body as she floated among them.

There was a dock nearby, and the swells breaking against its piers made a hollow walloping sound that was getting louder. Mary tried to open her eyes for a brief second, but the sun's rays were blinding, and she closed them again. In that second, she had seen the silhouette of a figure on the dock looking down at her.

She tried to open her eyes again to see who it was, but the light had dimmed and transformed into a bare bulb hanging in a hallway beyond the door. The door is open, and the silhouette from the dock framed in the doorway. The figure motionless at first moves into the room, and the door swinging shut, plunges the room into blackness.

Mary lying still, holds her breath, trying not to make a sound. She feels a slight vibration near her face an instant before her covers violently slide through her grip, the material rushing through her clenched fists. Mary, jerking away from the intruder, her motion causes her forehead to contact a freezing surface and wakes her from the dream. She found herself momentarily disoriented, her forehead pressed against the window of the car, still clutching the worn blanket in her lap.

After surfacing from sleep, she tried to push down the uncomfortable jumbled images of the dream. She could not help noticing as she looked out at the countryside the contrast between the darkness of the dream and the flat farmland and small islands of trees framed against a blue sky.

The steam whistle blew its familiar shrill, and a massive plume of white steam filled the air mixed with the black exhaust of the coal-fired engine — the signal, an indication that the train had reached its destination of Seven Lakes. The locomotive, six cars forward, entered into a sweeping turn, and the town had yet to come into view from Mary's car.

The train was traversing small trestle bridges across streams where the movement of water had frozen in place and would remain until the spring thaw.

She heard the rear door of her car slide open, and a conductor walking down the center aisle repeated "Seven Lakes, Seven Lakes." The conductor paused briefly beside Mary's seat, looking her over before moving through the rest of the car. She had become accustomed to men looking at her in a certain way, but it still made her uneasy when they did.

The train slowed, and Mary saw scattered houses along the edge of the town. Closer in, the residential streets had neat and orderly homes lining the Avenues, and even in the frigid cold, people were walking among the stores in the business district. The steam whistle blew several more times as the train approached the Seven Lakes Depot lying just ahead on the right side of the tracks.

Mary, looking out at the people who were gathering to meet the arriving train, couldn't believe she had finally arrived. When the train slowed to a stop, Mary experienced a sense of relief, and fear at the same time, and for a few moments, was unsure of what to do next.

CHAPTER 4

(Present)

Joel spent less than 30 minutes at his apartment, packing clothes and other items needed for his trip to Seven Lakes. He was still not used to living in his apartment home and did not enjoy spending time there.

He was recently divorced and living alone, a skill-set he was still trying to acquire after nearly 20 years of marriage. His tendencies toward work were more akin to an addiction, especially when it involved complex cases. Now, with nobody to go home to, he found work an easy escape.

He knew the futility of looking backward and learned hard lessons about the character of people through the unpleasantness of divorce. What he discovered is there are people in the world who are perfectly willing to shove you off the edge of a cliff if it will somehow benefit them.

Joel eased the Bel Air onto the entry ramp of the highway that would take him north, and away from the city. The asphalt was dry and chalky from the salt spread during a previous snowfall.

Once on the highway, he passed through several rings of suburbs before the scenery shifted to small Minnesota towns stitched together by a patchwork of farmland. He remembered taking this trip with his family as a child and having a feeling of embarking on a great adventure. The drive to Seven lakes always felt like it took forever, with the return trip to Minneapolis accomplished in a fraction of the time.

Joel's dad loved the outdoors and took every opportunity to trudge through woodlands, hand-drill holes into thick lake ice to fish in the dead of winter, or patiently sit adrift in a boat for hours waiting for an elusive Walleye to strike. Joel's appreciation of nature and the outdoors he credited to his dad.

Seven Lakes, a tourist town, had mostly small Mom & Pop resorts in the late 60s and 70s. They weren't resorts in the usual sense of the word; they were more like a string of rustic cabins with maybe a small store for supplies. The cabins, equipped with docks and small fishing boats, were designed to allow middle-class families an escape from the cities for a couple of weeks in the summer.

Joel looked over at his laptop bag, leaning against the passenger door. The top of the envelope containing Williams's letter was sticking out of one of its side pockets. He loved the processes involved with an investigation, grounded in logic, evidence, and facts. There was a sense of order to it all. It was something he had control over, something he could piece together through research. He would assemble the pieces one at a time building a case, and In the end, with luck, he might solve it or at least offer a probable solution.

The age of this cold case, however, would make the assembling process challenging. The information would be difficult to locate, memories will have faded, people will have moved away or died, and buildings and landmarks will have fallen victim to progress.

The thought of an outwardly innocuous town like Seven Lakes harboring the type of evil and danger, which could cause a young woman to lose her life, is the real mystery. Someone or something had caused her disappearance, and the letter, though vague on its surface, seemed to insinuate foul play.

CHAPTER 5

(Present)

Joel sat perfectly still. The only sound in the room, the labored breathing of the old man he had come to see. He could hear voices from the hallway that sounded far away and disinterested. Sunlight slanting in through partially open blinds caused patterns to dance on the wall above the bed's headboard.

He was disappointed when a nurse he met on the way to the room, informed him that Mr. William's dementia had progressed to a point where even rudimentary conversation was impossible.

He had spotted a small framed picture on Williams nightstand when he arrived and decided to take a closer look before leaving — making his way to the foot of the bed; he stopped for a few seconds before continuing along the left side toward the nightstand. Keeping an eye on the sleeping figure, he leaned down to pick up the picture. Williams' face was an unhealthy gray, covered in stubble. There was a dried white stain around his lower lip, and his breathing had become less labored. Joel could see the old man's eyes moving beneath heavily creased lids, and said half-aloud, "what did you see old man, what did you see?"

Joel studied the picture, two men standing side by side in front of a large home that looked to be one of the estates along shoreline drive. The photo, taken in the winter, showed a sparsely landscaped lot covered in snow. The home, a Tudor style, had the signature dark wood running between stucco that created the classic geometric designs accentuating pitched rooflines and framed windows.

As he studied the men's expressions, he had the sensation of being watched, and looking down at the old man, saw his eyes still closed. Looking back at the photograph, he saw something he had missed on his first inspection. Bringing the photo close to his face, he focused in on the right-side second-story window. There in the shadows, almost lost in the black and white graininess, a human-looking form hauntingly stared back at him.

He could tell the picture was of good quality, and he scanned its perimeter for any markings indicating a date or who the photographer might have been. Finding nothing, he looked back at the second story window where the image seemed to swirl among the varying shades of gray and black depending on the angle and amount of light hitting its surface. He could not say for sure it was a person, but in certain positions, it looked like someone standing in the shadows.

The picture frame was heavy and judging by its patina, made of silver. He turned the frame over and inspected the faded green felt backing. Four metal swivels held the backing to the frame, and he could tell from the worn felt, the assembly was taken apart many times in the past.

Joel slid the swivels clear and placing one hand on the felt, turned the frame over, releasing it from the frame. He carefully set the empty frame onto the stand before inspecting the photograph. There were some markings along the bottom-right edge of the picture which had been covered by the framework. Joel lifting the corner of the photo slightly from its backing, caused a small piece of fabric to slide from underneath and fall lightly to the floor.

The fabric turned out to be black lace with a floral design. There were bold dark lines outlining flowers and leaves with a delicate, almost transparent netting style weave between the patterns holding it together. The piece looked to have been cut or torn from something larger because three of its edges were uneven and frayed with the remaining side having a uniform finished look.

Setting the fabric next to the frame, he turned the photograph over. There were two names written on the back in an elegant flowing cursive style near the top edge. Gerald Swanson and Charles Patterson. The names meant nothing to Joel, but the picture and small piece of lace hidden inside changed his mind about leaving Seven Lakes just yet. Joel snapped a picture of the front and back of the photograph with his phone, placed the piece of lace into his shirt pocket, and after reassembling the frame, put it back in the same position he had found it.

It was nearly 4:00 PM, and he still needed a place to stay. Before leaving the nursing home, he decided to have a quick look at Williams's chart. He had noticed when he arrived that the facility had just one nurse's station on the main floor. A young girl who was attending the station, and mesmerized by her phone, had given Joel Williams's room number without any inquiries as to who he might be.

Joel made his way to the end of the hallway and down the stairs to the main lobby. When reaching the main level, he headed across the worn linoleum toward the nurse's station while keeping an eye on the girl. When she heard his footsteps and looked up, Joel glanced down at his watch while simultaneously quickened his pace. This time when he looked up, she was sitting straight, watching him approach. Reaching the station, he asked her for her name.

"Melody," she said with an inflection that made it sound like a question. Joel, in an even tone, said: "Melody, I am Dr. Gibbons from Minneapolis, and I have an urgent appointment back in the cities, I need to look at the current medications Mr. Williams is receiving."

Melody, looking relieved, knew where she could find the information and practically sprinted to the file cabinet to retrieve it.

Placing a thick folder on the counter, she returned to where she had been sitting. Joel scanned the face-sheet for the information he was seeking, and after finding it, slid the folder back across the counter, and thanked her for her assistance.

It had been nearly 40 years since Joel had been in Seven Lakes, and as he drove toward town and the lakeshore, memories of those times flooded in. Joel and his brothers had many adventures here, and for Joel, it had been a time of independence and freedom.

He drove down a quiet residential street toward the lake until it dead-ended into Shoreline Drive, turning right, he followed the natural curve of the Southside of the Lake toward the business district of Seven Lakes.

As he drove, he scanned the stately homes set-back on their lots and protected behind ornamental iron fences and privacy walls. He was looking for the Tudor from the photograph.

Joel remembered how he and his brothers would motor across the lake from their rented cabin, running their fishing boat close-in to the shore to look at the stately homes. In the opposite direction, near the outskirts of town, an abandoned ice harvesting operation spanned several acres of the shoreline. They had no idea at the time what the abandoned equipment might be, but the site became an irresistible place to be explored. A wooden structure rising from the edge of the lake looked like a roller coaster that had fallen into disrepair.

Joel had never visited the area during the winter months; summer tourism was the main driver for the area's economy. And judging by the lack of traffic on Shoreline Drive today, it probably still was.

Low clouds now blocking the sun, combined with a steady wind from the north, gave the day a raw unsettled feeling. He could see small patches of unmelted snow under heavily shaded areas of evergreens on the residential lawns.

He spotted the Tudor on a corner lot ahead and made a U-turn at the intersection to pull the Bel Air into a parking space on the lake-side of Shoreline Drive directly across from home. A wide grassy boulevard separated the road from a pedestrian sidewalk running near the shoreline. Joel stepping out into a cold wind off the lake, made his way down the embankment, across the walkway, and stood at the lake's edge.

He could feel the cold tumbling from the sky, permeating every inch of his body. The low clouds had moved in quickly and were pressing toward the ground, making the world seem smaller and darker. A feeling of snow was in the air, and he expected large flakes to appear at any moment. Looking toward the horizon, he saw the back edge of the cloud bank, where pale pink and purple ribbons of color ran horizontally through the small cloudless space.

Turning around, he looked back across at the Tudor. Structurally, it was the same house as in the picture. Trees and vegetation had matured over the years, and the lot looked considerably less barren. Looking up at the second-story windows, he could only see blackness there now. A sudden gust of wind sent an involuntarily shiver through his body, and he retreated up the incline to the warm interior of his car. Writing down the address of the Tudor in his notebook, he penned a reminder to check public records for the chain of title.

Joel pulled into the semi-circular drive of the Seven Lakes Grand hotel. The driveway finished in brick pavers aligned in a herringbone pattern. A portico built during the renovation complemented the original style of the old hotel. Joel parking near the front entrance tried to imagine what the scene may have looked like when Mary arrived from the train station. The hotel for Joel represented a tangible connection to her former life.

There was a high-end look to the hotel now, which had not been the case 40 years ago. Joel remembered the place looking run-down and perpetually in need of paint. According to an article he found online, the hotel had closed its doors in 1982 and, for the next 13 years, sat uninhabited except for vagrants who occasionally broke-in searching for shelter. On one such occasion, a trespasser nearly burned the place down, trying to stay warm by building a fire in a second-story room. Later, the hotel narrowly escaped the bulldozer before a New York firm purchased it a month before its scheduled demolition. The company that purchased it spent nearly a year renovating the property.

When Joel stepped out of his car, a sharply dressed man in uniform appeared on the sidewalk, briskly walking in his direction. "Can I take your luggage?" the man called out while surveying the classic lines of the Bel Air. Joel had only packed a small gym bag which he had already slung over his shoulder. Explaining this to the attendant, the young man seemed disappointed but perked back up when Joel asked about parking.

"Valet service is free for our guests," said the attendant.

"Great," Joel said, tossing him the keys. "Treat her gently."

Joel entered the hotel through metal-framed doors with beveled glass panes elegantly etched with the hotel's logo. The lobby was impressive, with variegated white marble floors, area rugs, and comfortable furniture arranged throughout. There were tall tropical plants and small palm trees ostensibly put in to provide a respite from the leafless vegetation and frigid winter temperatures of a Minnesota winter. Large arched windows facing the lake soared toward 20-foot ceilings, and multiple sets of French doors between the windows led out to walled-gardens, which he imagined were beautiful in the summer months.

A woman in a similar uniform as the valet stood behind the reservation counter to his left. She stared into a computer screen mounted into the surface of the desk and appeared to be typing on an invisible keyboard. The woman looked up and smiled as Joel approached. He noticed how the designer had used soft illumination to create a calming feel in and around the check-in area. The check-in process went smoothly, and Chelsea, the reservation specialist, was as pleasant as her smile. Joel was taken aback by the hotel's big-city prices, but the establishment looked to be first-class in every respect, and his room turned out to be no exception.

The opposite side of the lobby featured several businesses, likely added at the time of the renovation. Joel was happy to discover a coffee shop was one of them.

He could feel the day catching up with him as soon as he entered his fourth-floor room. The room featuring a king-sized bed, covered in a luxurious looking cream colored comforter, had more pillows than Joel had ever owned. Sitting on its edge, he leaned over on his side, only intending to rest for a few minutes, and immediately fell asleep. It turned out to be a fitful sleep where he felt cold, but could never muster enough energy to get under the covers.

The morning light streaming through the open curtains was disorienting at first, and it took him a couple of minutes to realize where he was. He heard the soft whirl of wheels in the hallway, and shortly after that, the smell of freshly brewed coffee. As soon as he could acquire some coffee for himself, he would be ready to dig into Mary's case.

CHAPTER 6
(December 1925)

The winter of 1925, had been a perfect season for the ice harvesting business in Seven Lakes. The lack of snow helped the ice obtain its proper thickness earlier than usual. The ice was checked daily by the Seven Lakes Ice Works leading up to harvest season, and the latest tests indicated it had reached its optimal thickness for harvesting.

The demand for the pure ice produced from Seven Lakes was on the rise, and the Company had experienced double-digit increases in shipped ice over the past several years. Seven Lakes, a spring-fed lake with a low mineral count, produced a crystal clear ice that was in high demand.

The railroads played an integral part in distributing ice from Seven Lakes to cities along their lines, and along with the ice shipped, local demand had also increased as the population of Seven Lakes continued to grow. There was a giant ice house that stored the blocks for the local community, and during the summer of 1925, the stored ice had run out for the first time that anyone could remember.

Two years prior, the company expanded the ice field, and it now encompassed close to a half-mile of shoreline and extending a quarter-mile out onto the ice. The harvest area formed a massive rectangle with its leading-edge only about a mile from the Main Street business district.

When the ice field expanded, the operation required more men to complete the harvest, which was a welcome byproduct since the area was an agricultural center, and work during winter months, scarce. The actual harvest could take two to three months and required a workforce of approximately 75 men. The wages were decent, the work dangerous, but it was a paycheck.

The operation was like a lot of other industries of the time, where the lions share of the profits ended up in the hands of people who did the least amount of work. It was usually a person with foresight who could insinuate himself into a position to benefit from the labors of others. In the case of the Seven Lakes Ice Works, that person was Charles Patterson.

Patterson, whose permanent home was in Minneapolis, was an independent broker for the railroad that operated in the northern territories. He had an unpleasant disposition and a reputation as a ruthless negotiator. People who knew him best said any idea which was not his, was automatically dismissed as if contrived by imbeciles. Patterson did not have real friends, just acquaintances who tolerated his toxic personality.

The railroad had a history of not making a profit in the small towns it connected and had gone bankrupt one time already. Patterson had taken it upon himself to change the equation for both the railroad and himself.

In 1922, Patterson put together a proposal he presented to the brass at the railroad's main offices in St. Paul. His plan was simple; negotiate better shipping rates for the railroad with the local merchants and farmers along its entire route. His proposed fee would be a tiny percentage of everything shipped under any new agreements he secured. For the railroad, it seemed like a no-lose scenario. The plan would not cost the company anything, at least not the way presented. Once approved, Patterson went to work traveling extensively between the railway towns and used his negotiating skills and understanding of human nature. His particular style of negotiations more closely resembled a bullying session rather than a healthy give and take.

Proposing the low percentage as his fee was a brilliant move, and as it turned out, one of the main reasons the railroad agreed to his proposal in the first place. Patterson made an insignificant amount from one deal, and nothing he could live on for ten deals, but as he worked tirelessly during the next year, he was able to secure over 100 agreements. At that point, the wealth potential of his plan began to emerge. A tiny piece of a vast stream of goods flowing from the northern tier of the nation made Charles Patterson a rich man. He had gained an impressive foothold, and there did not seem to be any limit to the personal wealth he could obtain as shipping volumes expanded each year.

Like a lot of rich men, though, Patterson was never satisfied. He did not give a second thought to the actual labor and toil involved in producing the goods; to him, they were numbers to manipulate to his advantage. The truth was, he enjoyed winning at any cost.

Patterson discovered the town of Seven Lakes early in his travels and found its amenities well suited for a summer home he had been contemplating building. The town's largest industry, the Ice Works, had been in operation since the mid-1800s, and the service relied heavily on the railroad to move the blocks of ice to larger cities where demand continued to grow.

Patterson successfully increased fees for the railroad for the 1924/25 season and again for the upcoming 1925/26 season. He had also worked out a deal whereby the owners of the Ice Works agreed to lease him some office space in their administrative building. The building overlooked the lake and the ice harvesting operation. This secondary headquarters for Patterson had come in handy in decreasing his travels to the cities. And when the time came, he had the advantage of supervising the construction of his new home on

Shoreline Drive. The office which Patterson lavishly furnished was on an otherwise empty second floor of the administration building.

Patterson, standing by the window of his office, looked out at the large checkerboard pattern of rectangles workers had scribed into the ice. Making the initial cuts was an essential first step in the harvesting operation, allowing for uniformity in the size of the blocks, which eventually get cut with powerful gas saws. The ice field stretched out almost as far as he could see, and it gave Patterson satisfaction to know he would earn compensation for every block hauled out of the freezing waters and shipped by rail. Only blocks the company stored in their icehouse escaped Patterson's higher fees, and he had not given up on finding a way to get a piece of that action too.

Patterson had little regard for relationships with the people he did business with, and was perfectly happy, and preferred to be alone. He knew the Seven Lakes Ice Works would ultimately make up for their added expenses by holding down wages for their workforce. Patterson had worked out the number in advance of the meeting and knew how much wiggle room the owners had. He always asked for a higher amount before falling back to his real number. His fall-back pricing gave owners the impression that it could have been worse, and that their objections kept the increase to a reasonable level.

Patterson watched a group of men working on the conveyor near the shoreline. The conveyor, extending several feet below the water's surface and powered by a large gas engine, grabbed the blocks with metal spikes to pull them from the water and place them onto the tramway.

The tramway rising from the water's edge followed the pitch of the bank. Once the land leveled off, the tram-way stretched another 200 feet or so across the yard. The blocks traveled along the tramway at an elevation of 6 to 8 feet above the ground. As the blocks approached the railroad spur, a diverter sent ice toward an awaiting boxcar or onto another branch of the tram for loading into the Ice House. At the end of the tramway, a reject diverter allowed operators to send imperfect blocks off the end of the tram, where they would freefall and crash onto a pile below. By the end of the season, the rejected ice blocks formed what looked like a gigantic sculpture glistening in the winter sun.

Patterson saw a lot of men milling about the entrance to the office building, the announcement that the harvest was getting underway had brought idle farmhands to claim their spots on a crew.

Patterson watched the operation for several minutes before losing interest and returning to his desk, where more productive activities awaited his attention. He was feeling good about the way things were going and thought it past time to enjoy some of the spoils of his success. What better time than the upcoming holidays to celebrate and indulge in his vices?

CHAPTER 7

(Present)

Distressed wooden floors with full columns clad in beveled mirrors created interesting angles and light patterns in the coffee shop connected to the hotel. It was still early, and customers already occupied many of the store's seating areas, their faces bathed in the unflattering light of electronic devices. Pictures hanging on the store's walls depicted scenes from Seven Lakes past. A large framed sepia-tone print behind the counter where employees scurried to keep up with customer orders showed an elevated view of the Seven Lakes train depot. A large number of people gathered near the tracks, women in dresses, and men in suits; a steam locomotive trailing passenger cars waited on the tracks, a cloud of steam partially obscuring its large drive wheels. Joel estimated the picture between 1910 and 1920 based on the clothes and model of cars parked on the street side of the depot.

He spotted another print hanging above a rack of branded coffee mugs and was surprised to be looking at a scene from his childhood. The picture pre-dated the time his family visited the area in the '70s, but the image the photographer had captured was from a familiar perspective. The photo, taken from the lake, was the same view he and his brothers saw when crossing the lake in their small motorboat.

The scene was depicting the Seven Lakes Ice Works from a time when it was still in operation. The Ice Works closed a few years before Joel and his brothers explored the site as kids. He remembered seeing the area for the first time from the lake, and his brother Mike guiding their boat into shore and cutting the motor when its bottom scraped sand and rock. Joel sitting in the bow, grabbed the anchor, and scrambling it ashore placed it several feet from the water's edge. He remembered the place making an impression on him as he stood near the boat surveying the site. It was eerily quiet, and there was something about the place Joel was unable to grasp at the time, but now believed it was a connection to the past the site represented. He stood in silence among the tall weeds, rusted motors, and elevated track and thought about the people who had once operated the equipment. He could imagine the noise, commotion, and busyness of the place and wondered why the workers had stopped coming.

The ruins were a fabulous discovery for Joel and his brothers, and they visited the spot often throughout several summer vacations and spent hours exploring and climbing on the old equipment. Looking back, Joel was pretty sure they must have been trespassing.

Joel ordered his usual latte and found a small round table with a bench seat against a sidewall. The store had a street entrance in addition to the hotel lobby, and he watched locals file in off Main Street for a respite from the bitterly cold morning. Other people entering the store from the hotel lobby dressed like winter did not exist in their world.

Somebody had left a copy of the Seven Lakes Chronicle on the far end of his bench seat, and scanning the headlines, he found one that sounded interesting in the lower right corner that read, "Four Local Boys Report Seeing Strange Light from Lake." Joel reaching over, picked up the paper to read the story.

According to the report, the boys venturing onto the ice around 5:30 PM this past Friday night had encountered strange light coming from underneath the ice. In northern climates in December, sunset is around 4:30 PM, so Joel knew it would have been dark on the ice, especially if there was no moonlight.

A boy named Jeff Brody said, "We spotted a small patch of ice from the distance that appeared to have light coming from underneath." The report went on to explain that shortly after reaching the spot, TJ Shaffer, the youngest boy in the group, went into hysterics about a face he saw in the ice. Brody and the other boys rushing to the spot were unable to see anything unusual. The older boys concluded TJ's imagination had gotten the best of him.

When questioned about their location, the boys were unsure about their distance from the shoreline but believed they were nearly parallel with the section of Shoreline Drive that housed the abandoned warehouses. They stated the mysterious light disappeared after they arrived at the location. Brody went on to say that "when the light went away, the ice looked like every other part of the frozen lake."

Officials at the Police Department dismissed the incident as an attempt by the boys to revive the local "Ice Lady." Legend. Joel wrote the reporter's name in his notebook.

Buttoning up his jacket, so it covered his neck, Joel stepped out on to Main Street to have a look at the downtown after his 40-year absence. Turning up the sidewalk, he headed away from the lake. Being here felt right to him, almost as if predestined. He knew the past was all around him, hidden behind facades, in ashes of long-ago fires and buried under decades of progress.

Joel assumed one of the two men in front of the Tudor was the owner. He would check the courthouse records and also lookup Mr. William's previous address listed in his file at the nursing home. The date of Williams admission to the facility was over ten years ago, which meant he had written his letter shortly after reading about the missing girl in Minneapolis.

Before leaving his hotel room, Joel placed the lace fabric found inside the picture frame into a small plastic ziplock bag and then put the plastic bag inside a standard mailing envelope, which he addressed to his friend Marty. Marty could have the crime lab take a look at the fabric. He hoped they would be able to discern its approximate age by analyzing its construction and composition.

Spotting a book store on the opposite side of the street, Joel crossed over to see if it was open. The store, Leisure Time Book Sellers, had an inviting entrance with two display windows extending beyond its façade. In one window, recent best-sellers staged on a small table alongside a comfy leather chair, a pair of glasses on a side table, and a faux fireplace. Colorful watercolor artwork hung in the opposite window. One is showing wildflowers in an open field with an imposing castle in the distance. The title asked, "Where Would You like to Go Today?"

Joel pulled the brightly painted red door open and heard an old-timey bell attached to a spring announce his arrival. The inside of the store was cozy with tastefully arranged furniture creating reading nooks in and around the bookshelves. The light-colored wood shelves and brightly lit space invited readers to take their time.

The store at first appeared empty until a short, middle-aged woman with a boyish style haircut burst through a door in the back. The woman, dressed in faded jeans and a white button-down shirt, had a pair of maroon-colored glasses hanging from a silver chain. Her demeanor was high-energy when she greeted Joel.

"Is there anything I can help you find?" She asked. Joel learned her name was Elizabeth, but she preferred Beth, she was not the owner, but had been there nearly five years and was a life-long resident of Seven Lakes before he had a chance to respond to her first question.

"I was wondering," Joel hesitated, "if you have any books on the legend of the Ice Lady?" Beth seemed politely amused by the question.

"No, I don't believe I have ever seen anything written specifically on that topic," Beth replied, "the story, I believe, is loosely based on a woman who went missing in a snowstorm sometime in the early 1900s."

"What's the legend?"

"Same as most of these types of legends, if someone sees her, it is a precursor to something bad. With the Ice Lady, it signals a severe winter storm. Details about the real person who vanished are sketchy," Beth added.

"Have there been sightings?"

"Not many that I can remember," she paused, "there is one interesting thing about the reports, though."

"What's that?"

"The people who have reported sightings are not your usual suspects. I mean," she paused, "people you wouldn't expect to go in for that type of thing. You know, respectable and all that." Joel nodded that he understood.

"The sightings have supposedly occurred near the lakeshore, and sometimes were followed by storms, but people are skeptical with modern-day forecasting. It tends to take a lot of the supernatural out of weather predictions and probably is not as impressive as it might have been in the past."

"Maybe she will show up this week; the weather looks to be deteriorating," Joel said with a smile.

"Maybe." Beth agreed.

Joel showed her the picture of the two men in front of the Tudor on his phone. "Do you have any idea who these two men are?" Joel asked, handing her his phone.

Beth, looking at the picture, shook her head, "no, I don't recognize them, but there is a woman in town, kind of a self-appointed historian of Seven Lakes, I am sure she would know or could find out."

"Where would I find her?"

"She's a volunteer at the Seven Lakes Historical Society, actually just a few blocks from here, I would call first though. The place has irregular hours."

Joel thanking her before leaving the warmth of the store returned to the gray cold of Main Street, where the mean temperature hovered in the teens. Once back outside, he noticed the skies had grown darker, and the dismal light filtering through the clouds gave the town a tired look.

Turning back in the direction of the lake, he walked into the biting wind that had previously been to his back. As far as he could tell, the downtown had not changed much in 40 years. Businesses had come and gone, but it was the same old buildings and storefronts from his youth.

When he reached the corner of Main and Shore Line Drive, he looked across the frozen surface of Seven Lakes. The wind off the ice stung his exposed face, and when he placed his hands on his cheeks, he felt the stubble from two days without shaving. He thought about Mary leaving the warmth and safety of the hotel to venture out into a storm for what reason?

He had a faint recollection of a dream from the previous night, where a young woman gazed at him from a distance. It had been a brief encounter before she disappeared into a veil of white.

Something about standing on this corner had triggered the memory, and he looked across at the Seven Lakes Grand, the last place she reportedly was seen.

He remembered experiencing a feeling of helplessness when the woman disappeared from view, and that same feeling came over him now as he looked across at the hotel.

Joel's investigative method had always started with familiarizing himself with known locations a missing person frequented. He wondered in a case as old as Mary's if his usual methods would still prove useful. The only other site he knew for sure she had been was the train station where she arrived.

CHAPTER 8

(December 5, 1925)

The steam locomotive approaching Seven Lakes was a thing of beauty for Jim Braden. Most people had become accustomed to the hulking engines pulling their cargos of people and supplies and rarely paid them much attention. Still, for Braden, the Seven Lakes Station Master, he never tired of the magnificent iron beasts with their rhythmic steam propulsion and all of their hissing, knocking, and ticking noises even when sitting still.

The Seven Lakes station, built at street level, had an expanse of dirt between the tracks and station house, and during a hard rain, the area turned into a quagmire of mud. Several people who waited inside the station, now reluctantly made their way into the cold to greet their parties.

The locomotive slowed to a crawl passing in front of the station, the engine coming to a full stop just before the tracks crossed Main Street. A powerful release of steam in and around the large drive wheels sounded like the engine sighing in relief of arriving.

Porters appeared outside the station house and sliding open doors of an attached storage garage, pulled out two carriage style flat-bed luggage carts. The porters steered the carts toward the luggage car, where they began retrieving luggage and transferring it to the waiting transportation. Several cars lined up in the front of the station were waiting to take passengers to their final destination.

Braden had been the Station Master at the Seven Lakes depot for over 15 years and was the most knowledgeable person in town about the comings and goings of Seven Lakes inhabitants and outsiders. Looking across the lobby at the official station clock, he noted the arriving train from Fairview had come to a stop at 11:04 AM. The trains in these parts usually ran on time unless there was some unforeseen calamity. For Braden, 11:04 was as good as on time. He watched the passengers stepping down from the cars as the porters loaded the luggage carts.

Filling in the official logs with his neat hand printing, Braden recorded arrival times, departure times, and the number of ticketed passengers. In his head, he kept his unofficial log, where he listened for good gossip he could share. His favorite method for sharing was through the town's switchboard and the ladies who worked for the phone company in the basement of The Seven Lakes Grand Hotel.

Braden's office projected beyond the main structure giving him an unobstructed view of both arriving and departing trains. Closing his log-book, he slid it onto a shelf behind his desk. Glancing down the track, where the passenger cars were now mostly empty, he was surprised to see a young woman stepping off the second to last car. She looked to be traveling alone, and once she stepped from the train, she hesitated, like she was unsure of what to do next. Braden could tell even from this distance; she wasn't a typical traveler who claimed Seven Lakes as their destination. There was something about her that looked a little too polished for small-town Minnesota.

Braden relished his role as the gatherer of information; it gave him a sense of importance when people were eager to hear what he had to say. Today's arrival of the young woman traveling alone was just the kind of good story he could embellish and nudge his listeners into their preconceived prejudices.

A porter rounding the corner of the station after unloading luggage into the cars spotted the woman Braden was observing. She was still several cars down the tracks, moving slowly toward the station. Parking his cart near the station house, the porter headed in her direction to offer assistance. Braden watched the interaction, and after the two briefly talked, she continued toward the station house.

As she came closer, Braden could see his assessment had been right. The woman, smartly dressed, wore a dark blue overcoat buttoned up the front, knee-high lace-up boots, a tan scarf, and a small black cap tilted forward with a feather adornment. Her short black hair curled forward from underneath her hat, perfectly framed her high cheekbones.

Braden couldn't remember a time he had ever seen someone quite so lovely; her pale skin looked soft and youthful with just a touch of color in her cheeks. She wore dark lipstick that accentuated the delicate nature of her fair skin. When she saw Braden watching her through the window, she smiled. It was a beautiful smile that caught him off guard, and he quickly pretended to busy himself with imaginary paperwork. Braden would need to find out her story because it would not be long before people started talking. A moment later, looking up from his desk, he saw there were no more passengers along the tracks, and he assumed the woman had made her way toward the waiting transportation.

The porter who had engaged the woman was over near a partially loaded cart next to the luggage car. As he looked through luggage, he paused every so often to rub his hands together for warmth. After a short time, he pulled a bag that matched the one the woman carried. Braden watched as he disappeared alongside the station carrying her bag.

Loading the woman's luggage into a car with the "Seven Lakes Grand Hotel" painted on its side, he signaled the driver to go, with a bang on the side of the vehicle. The driver maneuvered the car slowly through deep ruts frozen in the road, before turning toward Shoreline Drive.

When the porter returned to the station, Braden left his desk and went into the main lobby to intercept him. The porter's name was Rodney, and he had only been on the job for about two months. When Rodney saw Braden heading in his direction, Rodney, retraced his steps, hoping he had not done anything wrong. Despite having the Station Master bearing down on him, he was thankful for the warmth inside the station and nervously rubbed his hands together as he watched Braden approach. When Braden was still several feet away, Rodney, in an anxious voice, asked if he could be of assistance.

"Yes, the passenger, uh, the young girl," Braden hesitated. Rodney, relieved that the question was about the woman, quickly filled the awkward moment, "yes," he said, "her name is Mary, and she is traveling alone. I was surprised she had no idea where to stay, and she said she had no family or acquaintances in the area. I told her she would be in good hands at the Seven Lakes Grand Hotel and helped her with transport to the hotel."

Braden, listening to the information, showed no visible reaction, but also thought the woman's situation strange. "Carry-on," he said, abruptly ending the conversation by turning and walking in the opposite direction.

Braden would make some inquiries of the Station Master in Fairview to see what, if anything, he might know. In the meantime, her story would make for some intriguing gossip where his audience would have wide latitude to speculate about her intentions.

CHAPTER 9

(Present)

Joel could see faint light seeping in around the edges of the fabric blinds of his hotel room. The light increased in intensity as minutes passed, but he was still too tired to get up. It was his second morning in Seven Lakes, and he could hear cars on Main Street as the town started to come to life.

Barely awake, his mind shifted to the case as he anticipated his unannounced visit to the police department. He planned to give local authorities a heads up about being in town. Let them know he was on official business and all, well sort of, he didn't have a real client. Small towns were notorious for gossip, and he guessed it wouldn't take long for people of Seven Lakes to know his business after the visit.

An hour later, leaving through the hotel's front entrance, he walked one block in the opposite direction of the lake, crossed the street and turned left down a side street that shielded him from bitterly cold wind.

The municipal building encompassing the Seven Lakes police department was only three blocks from the hotel, and Joel covered the distance in less than five minutes.

The building, an imposing brick structure, had all the hallmarks of being built during President Roosevelt's "New Deal." Joel's high school, built during that same period, had that specific look like the same architectural firm had designed all of the buildings during that era. The interior of this building was spacious with shiny terrazzo floors, wide hallways, and 12-foot ceilings. The offices had transom windows that would have provided ventilation before air conditioning. The frosted glass on the doors had old-style gold lettering outlined in black. But the best thing for Joel was the building was warm.

The police department on the directory showed it to be on the second floor, and Joel decided to take the stairs with the ornate railings rather than chance the small elevator that looked to be a couple of decades past its prime. When reaching the top landing, he saw the familiar police badge design on a set of double doors at the end of the hallway.

The main room of the department as he stepped inside was an open space with five desks without partitions. The desks lined up in two rows behind a short railing looked like the kind used in courtrooms. The room might have once functioned as a courtroom, old government buildings routinely repurposed, space and departments made do with what was available.

There wasn't a receptionist, and a man in street clothes who Joel presumed to be a detective, stood inside a doorway at the back of the room. The man is calling across to Joel, offering his assistance. He was young, probably in his early thirties with curly close-cropped hair, dressed in grey pants, a matching vest, and a white button-down shirt, open at the collar.

Joel, not thrilled with communicating across a room, shouted, "My name is Joel Vick, I am a private detective from Minneapolis. I am looking for information on a missing person cold case." Joel paused, to let the detective digest the information. The detective, deciding the info was critical enough to make the trek across the room, walked over to where Joel stood at the short railing, stuck out his hand, and introduced himself as detective Sims. Joel shook his hand.

"I am not aware of an open missing person case."

"I know it's an old cold case."

Sims studying, Joel, for a few seconds, asked, "how can I help?"

Joel explained that before taking the liberty of launching an investigation, he made it his policy to alert local authorities of his activities. Sims politely listened, and then as if losing interest said, "Chief Swanson should be in at any minute if you would like to wait."

"I would," Joel said as he thought about the two names on the back of the photograph, and wondered if there was any relation. Joel found a seat on his side of the railing, and just as he was about to sit down, A short, stocky man with powerful shoulders and arms disguised under a neatly pressed suit pushed open the outer door. The man looked to be about Joel's age and wore an expression of someone used to dealing with problems. When he spotted Joel, his face indicated Joel might be one of those problems.

Joel introduced himself and, with minimal detail, explained the purpose of his visit. Swanson's expression relaxed somewhat as he walked through the opening in the railing and motioned for Joel to follow. "Come to my office," Swanson said as he made his way toward the doorway where Sims had been standing earlier.

Joel sat down in one of two wooden straight back chairs in front of the Chief's desk and wondered if they were purposely selected for their lack of comfort to discourage people from staying too long.

"So," Swanson said, "who's missing?" Joel, looking directly at the Chief, said, "Mary Benton." The name was familiar to the Chief, and the recognition swift, like the shutter of a camera.

Swanson looking across at Joel for a few seconds, leaned forward in his chair and said, "Joel, do you mean to tell me our little story about some local boys seeing weird stuff out on a frozen lake made it to the Minneapolis, and you came up to investigate?"

"No," Joel said, "I am following up on a letter I received in my office a couple of days ago."

"A letter?'

"Yeah, sent by a resident here in Seven Lakes indicating there was new information about her disappearance." Joel thought it interesting the Chief drew a connection to Mary Benton from the recent incident on the ice.

The original expression the Chief had when he arrived returned, and Joel's information was not what he had expected to hear.

"A letter," Swanson said, this time making a statement that he punctuated with raised eyebrows.

"Yes, the author stated he was the last person alive who knew something about her disappearance." Swanson assumed whoever wrote the letter would be a confidential source if they were a client. Swanson leaning back in his chair, looked at Joel as if he were obstructing the Chief's routine.

"Joel," he finally said, "the Mary Benton case has got to be over 90 years old."

"I know," Joel said with a resigned tone.

Something switched in Swanson's demeanor that suggested it was time for him to move on to other issues. The Chief, while eyeing the stack of paperwork on his desk, said, "Joel, I appreciate you letting us know about your investigation, Sims can assist you with any information our department might have. I doubt there is much in the way of records, but you are certainly welcome to look."

Joel, feeling like the conversation was over, stood and thanked Swanson before walking back into the main room where Sims huddled in discussion with another detective. As Joel approached, Sims held up a finger to the other detective and walked over to intercept him. Joel explained the Chief had assigned Sims to help locate any records related to the Mary Benton cold case. Sims nodded, "So, where would one find old cold case files around here?" Joel asked.

Sims explained that they stored all inactive files in the basement within a locked storage area as well as collected evidence from on-going investigations.

"Give me a minute; I will take you down," Sims said as he walked back to the desk to finish his conversation with the other detective.

Joel imagined a dark, cobwebby space tucked away in the bowels of the old building where nobody voluntarily ventured.

Sims did not have an aversion to using the old elevator, and Joel not wanting to show his apprehension, took his place beside him in the tiny space. When the doors opened in the basement, Joel was pleasantly surprised by the well-lit area and polished concrete floors. He saw a chain-link fence toward the back wall and walking to the cage, Sims opened the padlock holding the chain and unwrapped it from the permanent post allowing the door to swing inward.

Sims led the way down one of four aisles between evidence shelves that were at least eight feet tall and ran for approximately 30 feet. The shelves, populated with mostly clear plastic bins, had laminated sheets with numbers taped to their outsides. When they reached the back wall, Sims looking back at Joel said, "if it's old and we have it, it will be in one of these cabinets."

Joel looked at the row of mismatched file cabinets that resembled a timeline into the past. Somebody had created a date range with a Dynamo embosser and affixed the red labels to each cabinet. Joel, walking to the far corner, examined the oldest looking cabinets until he found one with the date range of 1920 – 1925. Sliding out the top drawer, he saw it was about three-quarters full. Spotting a separator tab near the rear of the drawer labeled 1925, Joel found two files. Pulling out one of the two manila envelopes, he saw it had a couple of rubber stamp marks along with the words "missing person" printed across the front. Joel turned to look at Sims, who had been watching him.

"You were not kidding about a cold case," Sims said, before taking a couple of minutes to explain the rules of the evidence room. As Sims was leaving, he paused partway down between the shelving to ask Joel if he needed anything else. Joel assured him he would lock-up when finished. Joel was pretty sure it was against department policy for him to be left alone in the evidence room, but small towns tended to operate under more casual rules.

Joel looking at the faded manila envelope in his hands, turned it over a couple of times to read the markings and writing on its outside. Unwinding the brittle string holding the top flap, he slid the contents onto a table positioned below a fluorescent fixture. He noticed the person who initially filled out the paperwork had neat and orderly handwriting that looked more like printing even though some of the characters connected.

The case number MP112 was at the top of the report, and the name Mary Benton printed on the first line. The date was December 23, 1925. The time of the report was 3:00 PM. The person who had called in the report was a Mr. Talbot, whose position the report listed as manager of the Seven Lakes Grand Hotel. The information was taken at the hotel by a Sgt. Ross.

According to Talbot, several hotel employees were unable to make it into work that day, and the remaining staff had fallen behind on many of the duties associated with running the hotel. Martha Teal, a maid who cleaned the fourth-floor rooms and who was familiar with Mary's routine, was surprised when Mary didn't answer her door that morning. Martha thought she might be in the dining room and cleaned the rest of the rooms on the floor before returning to Mary's room.

Around 1:00 PM, Martha finished cleaning the rest of the rooms and returned to Mary's room, again knocking on her door. Getting no answer, she used her pass-key and found Mary's belongings still in place, but no sign of Mary. Martha believed it an unusual circumstance and decided to tell Mr. Talbot. Talbot surveyed the staff after talking with Martha and found that no one had seen Mary that morning. Still unsure of the seriousness of the matter, Talbot decided to notify the police. Sgt. Ross was assigned and arrived at the hotel around 3:00 PM.

Using a blank sheet of notebook paper as an unofficial inventory sheet, Ross listed the items in Mary's room. The page, titled "Mary Benton, Room 413."

1. Hair-brush
2. Glass perfume bottle
3. 2 Dresses
4. Pair of shoes
5. Locket with picture
6. Advertisement for Seven Lakes
7. Small mirror
8. Ticket stub from the railroad
9. Empty suitcase
10. Assorted undergarments and socks
11. Assorted soaps

Joel, reading the list, thought it strange that she barely had any possessions. The fact that she had an advertisement for Seven Lakes was also noteworthy. The index for Joel brought her to life; she was no longer just a newspaper account. There was a bin number on the form, which probably meant, at some point, the police collected the items from her room as evidence. Joel did not have any illusion the bin had survived.

Joel read through the interviews, Sgt. Ross conducted. Martha explained that Mary, during her prolonged stay at the hotel, seldom left her room. After surveying the staff, Talbot checked her account with the front desk and found she had paid up through December 29.

The report also described Sgt. Ross's room inspection. Mr. Talbot, an unnamed Bellhop, and Sgt. Ross went to the room together, and using a master key to enter, allowed Sgt. Ross to inspect the room and itemize its contents. Sgt. Ross notated the placement of the items within the room, stating the perfume bottle and hair-brush were on the dressing table, two dresses were hanging in the closet, and a pair of shoes were under the writing desk. There were some assorted undergarments within a dresser drawer along with some bath soaps.

Sgt. Ross summarized his findings at the bottom of the page. He indicated there was no evidence of a rushed departure and that, in his opinion, she had every intention of returning. Ross added a final sentence that seemed to illustrate his frustration about the overall lack of information about Mary. He wrote, "Mary Benton, arriving by train on December 5, 1925, from Fairview, took up residence at the Seven Lakes Grand on that same day. According to staff, Mary did not appear to have either family or friends in the local area and throughout her prolonged stay, mostly kept to herself. A hotel employee recalls seeing her leave the hotel on the evening of December 22, 1925, amid a severe snowstorm. Her intended destination was unknown, and as of the time of this report, she has not returned.

There were two other people Sgt. Ross interviewed the following day as staff trickled back in the aftermath of the storm. Betty Samson, a dining room worker, who saw Mary at breakfast most days, had talked with her for short periods during those times. Jimmy Deal, a bellboy who told the manager about a man who earlier in the day, asked about how he could get a note to Mary. According to Deal, the man had shown up at the same time as travelers from the train station and told Jimmie he had a message for Mary from the haberdashery on Main Street.

Betty explained she had seen Mary descend the main staircase and leave the hotel just before 7:00 PM on the night of the storm. She was sure of the time because it was the end of her shift. According to Betty, Mary was wearing a long coat and a black cap. Betty went on to say even though they talked during breakfast, she felt like Mary was a private person, and Betty was not one to pry. She did think it odd at the time when Mary left the hotel into deteriorating conditions but did not think any more about it that night.

For Joel, the Bellboy's story was the most interesting, but there was not anything in the file beyond his initial interview. He did not see where any follow up was completed. He understood the town and police were likely overwhelmed with problems associated with the storm; by all accounts, it had placed terrible hardships on an enormous swath of the state. Maybe, there just weren't enough resources to look for a missing person who nobody seemed to know anyway.

Jimmie Deal explained to Sgt. Ross how he was busy sorting luggage brought in by the new arrivals from the train station. A man from behind him said he had a note to deliver to a young woman named Mary. Jimmie, like every other male in the hotel, knew of Mary. A woman with her looks didn't come around Seven Lakes that often. Jimmie gave the man her room number, hoping to avoid making the trip himself. The man thanked him and went on his way. Jimmie said he never looked up from his work but remembered the man's shoes looked expensive.

Joel leaning over the table, put his upper body weight on his hands and arms, and hovered above the papers. It was if he was trying to will additional information from the incomplete investigation. It was apparent the note was an essential missing piece of the puzzle, and Joel doubted the man's story because she had taken the letter with her into the night.

He stared at the reports ledger where dates and times of interviews had been conducted in chronological order and noticed the last entry was three days after Ross completed the primary interviews. In the notes section to the right of the date was a confusing two-word entry, "Unreliable Witness." What did that mean? Someone else came forward? Had someone seen something? Why had the person been deemed unreliable? It was a frustrating entry when considering the overall lack of follow-through on the case. Someone had gone to the trouble of pulling the file, writing in the date and then made a decision that the information for whatever reason was not relevant, or the person not credible.

Glancing at his watch, he was surprised at how much time had passed. He gathered up the old paperwork and slipping it back into the envelope, tied the brittle string around the big brown buttons to secure the flap. He placed the file back into the wooden filing cabinet and slid the door closed.

Joel believed Mary was somewhere in Seven Lakes. It was unreasonable to think she could have gone far in the storm. Mr. Williams witnessed something, and on the very day of her disappearance, a mysterious note delivered to her room. The file, although incomplete, had strengthened his determination to find out what happened to her.

Joel took the rickety elevator back to the main floor when he was unable to locate the staircase. Taking another look at the directory, he headed down the hallway in search of the Registrar of Deeds office. Joel needed to check on the chain of title for the Tudor and also take a look at the property card with the address listed on Williams file in the nursing home. He found the Registrar office near the end of the hallway, and a pleasant woman who appeared to be in her fifties greeted him as he entered. After explaining what he was looking for, she showed him a set of cabinets that looked suspiciously like old card catalogs used in libraries. The woman told him how they filed the properties and that there would be a separate card for each owner of a particular property. The cards have reference numbers relating to plat and deed information, and that information is in large hardbound books also located in this office.

The cards were in alphabetic order by street name and then in numeric ascending order by address. It only took Joel a few minutes to find the Tudor once he had the right drawer, 500 Shoreline Drive. There were four cards for the home, and as he flipped to the back card, he moved the first card up to mark the spot. The recording date was November 1922, and a purchase price of $225.00 appeared to be for the lot, which was nearly three acres in size. The purchaser, Charles Patterson, was one of the two men listed on the back of the old photo. The next card showed improvements to the property, the addition of a house in 1925 with a value of $6000.00.

A subsequent purchaser acquired the property in 1928 for a recorded sales price of $15,000, and in 1958 the property sold to its current owner for $98,500. Joel took pictures of the two Patterson cards with his phone before replacing them in the order he found them.

Next, he searched the property shown on the medical file for Mr. Williams and found the current owner on the first card. Behind the first card, there was a blank card with a large red stamp that read "TAX SALE." The card behind that showed that the county had foreclosed on the property in 1995 for delinquent taxes. As far as Joel could tell, the taxes had remained unpaid for at least ten years at the time of the foreclosure. The property was in the name of Mr. Williams when the foreclosure took place.

CHAPTER 10.

(December 21, 1925.)

It was a classic winter's night in Seven Lakes, clear skies, calm winds, and invigorating cold. A local farmer who owned a horse-drawn sleigh was hired by the Seven Lakes Grand Hotel to take guests out onto the frozen lake or if there was snow, along Shoreline Drive. The owner of the sleigh fastened bells to the reigns adding a festive sound in the night air. The hotel, its lights ablaze, looked like a jewel poised on the edge of the lake and could be seen from distant shores.

The holiday season in Seven Lakes was nearing its pinnacle, and the Grand Hotel, the center of the town's social scene, had celebrations scheduled through the New-year. New arrivals pushed the hotel's occupancy to near capacity.

Mary's room had a view of the lake, but she hardly noticed. The room was a place of refuge where she escaped the world for, however, temporarily a time. Tomorrow would be her 17th day staying at the hotel, and with money running out, she still had no prospect of securing work. She spent every waking hour fearful about the day she would have to leave.

Lying in her bathtub, she slid down under the warm water until her chin was even with its surface. Being submerged gave her a sense of security like she was invisible to the world. There was a draft in her room, and she could feel the cold air against her exposed face. The only sound in the room, a hollow Ker-plop as drops from the spigot, sent tiny ripples across the water's surface.

She tried to imagine herself within the scene depicted on the Seven Lakes travel poster as she had so many times in the past. Everything in her imagination consisted of lush greens and crisp blues. Sometimes the colors intermingled into differing shades and densities and moved in patterns like peering through a kaleidoscope. Bright yellow light penetrating between the edges of color was warm against her skin, and worry flowed from her body.

Mary's memories of Christmas from the road with her mother were small fleeting moments, where strangers went out of their way to show kindness. She neither understood the cause of their generosity nor saw it repeated at other times of the year. She did not count memories from the foster home because her life had effectively ended with the death of her mother.

Mary awoke abruptly, submerged and shivering. The warmth of the water dissipated, left the tub cold and inhospitable. Disoriented, she clutched the topsides and pulled herself from beneath the water, the cold air clinging to her wet skin. Bracing herself with one arm, she climbed over the side of the tub and grabbed a towel from the back of a chair. Wrapping herself into the material, she tried to cover as much exposed skin as possible. Standing there partially naked, she could hear the soft chatter of her teeth as shivers moved through her in waves.

Despite her anxiety about the hotel's Christmas Celebration, she forced herself to dress, fighting off the temptation to get into bed and hide beneath the covers.

When finished dressing, she put on her simple jewelry and sparingly dabbed perfume behind her ears from a nearly empty bottle. The fragrance belonged to her mother, and Mary had watched her each night preparing to go out for the evening. The smell of the perfume was like having her in the room again.

The celebration, scheduled to start at 6 pm, and Mary, ready early, went down to find an inconspicuous place near the fire to watch guests arrive. She was surprised to see how the staff had transformed the lobby when she reached the final flight of stairs. The hotel had added several fresh-cut evergreens nearly ten feet in height decorated with glass ornaments, ribbon, and large pine cones.

Near the center of the room, a glistening block of ice was sitting on a sturdy looking table where later, a sculptor artist would demonstrate his skill in transforming it into a replica of the hotel. The Seven Lakes Ice Works provided the ice and sponsored the sculptor. Mary walking near the table, marveled at the clarity of the ice block and the way reflected the room's lights. Bending down and putting her face close, she felt an invisible band of cold emanating from its surface. Looking through the block, she loved how everything appeared fluid, like an impressionist painting, where the light was diffused and soft. Mary, mesmerized with the scene, smiled at the thought of living in such a place.

By 6 pm, guests gathered in the lobby and front hallway. The kitchen staff set out hot cider in glass bowls and people who came in from the cold, sipped the cider while using the cup to warm their hands. A bright birch wood fire added warmth to the room, its flames reflecting across the polished wooden floor.

Mary could hear the conversation of two couples who had moved closer to the fire. They talked about the weather and the lack of snow this season. Mary, not wanting to be noticed, pre-occupied herself by periodically glancing toward the entry, as if her party was arriving at any minute.

The faces of the people who turned down her requests for work were still vivid in her memory, and she searched the faces in the room to see if any were present now. The encounters had left her feeling like an outsider with nothing of value to offer. She sensed a hostile attitude like she had been stigmatized, especially by women. It reminded her of the way people treated her mother during the last couple of years of her life.

The festivities in the hotel built with each new arrival, and the activity swirling around Mary reinforced her isolation. She could hardly believe the unease she felt on the inside, did not somehow manifest itself outwardly. Still, the people closest to her seemed oblivious to both her situation and existence.

Mary, on some level, understood her plan to start a new life in Seven Lakes had failed. Her imagination of the place skewed by smart advertising images had sold her an unobtainable dream. She could not have known about underlying forces of exclusion, prejudices, and suspicions. She was an outsider, stigmatized by her past, and falsely accused by innuendo.

Mary had witnessed her mother escaping plenty of tight situations. She always seemed to have the last card to play. That was, of course, until her hand ran out in that faraway town overlooking a lake so large, you couldn't see the opposite shoreline. Mary, however, didn't believe she possessed the same courage or inner strength to take care of herself if backed into a corner.

CHAPTER 11

(Present)

The Seven Lakes Chronicle building had the look of a small-town newspaper trying to survive in a digital age of fast news cycles, and skittish advertisers questioning the value of print. Joel could see by the size of the office; it had once housed a larger workforce. Today, there was only Mark Sorenson, sitting alone at his desk just beyond the reception area.

Joel had written Sorenson's name in his note pad after reading the article about the young boys seeing the strange light on the ice. Sorenson looked to be in his fifties, with a full head of dirty blond hair, a dark tan that looked purchased, and an open, friendly smile.

"You must be Joel," Mark said, getting up and walking over to greet him. "Welcome to our humble establishment. I have to admit, I've wanted to talk with you since I heard about your investigation."

"Where did you hear about my investigation?"

Mark smiled, "I do have an advantage of being in the business, but since your visit to the police department, your investigation was pretty much on the street." Mark invited Joel over to his desk and, along the way, asked how he could be of help.

"I am interested in the article you wrote about the boys seeing the strange light."

"Really?" Mark said, sounding surprised.

"I know it's a bit weird, but reading between the lines, I felt like you were giving the story some credence. What did you make of the boy's story?"

"They did come across as credible. I guess as a journalist, the amount of detail they provided impressed me. I have covered fake reports; this had a different vibe."

"Hmm"

"So tell me, how does a detective from Minneapolis end up in Seven Lakes investigating a cold case?"

"By invitation, I received a letter."

"A letter?"

Joel could tell Sorenson's interest was piqued. "From a Mr. Williams, who as it turns out, is too far along with Dementia to provide any additional context or detail to his otherwise cryptic letter. He looks to be near death lying in the Seven Lakes County Nursing Home."

"How did he manage to write a letter?"

"Good question, it turns out; it was written ten years before being sent."

"What?" Sorenson looked confused.

"An orderly found it inside of Williams bible when straightening his room. Turned it into the nursing station, and since it was addressed and sealed, they put a stamp on it, and stuck it in the mail."

"That's crazy," Sorenson said, seeing the potential story. "I want an exclusive when you solve the case."

Joel smiled, "You mean IF I solve the case."

"What did the letter say?"

"Essentially, he witnessed something as a boy having to do with Mary's disappearance, and that the matter had weighed on him his entire life."

Sorenson emitted a low whistle, "I suppose you already know that the two Schafer kids who were on the ice that night are his grandsons?

Now it was Joel's turn to be surprised."You're kidding?"

"No, old man Williams got married late in life to a girl half his age and had a daughter. His wife left him with the child a few years later. He never recovered, couldn't hold a job, got heavily into the bottle. He was the town drunk for decades."

"The daughter?"

"Seems to have done OK despite her childhood. Moved away as soon as she was able to. She returned thirty years later with a husband and two young children shortly after they placed Williams into the Nursing Home."

"What's the story on the *Ice Lady* reference by the police?"

"I believe the story is a bit of a hybrid."

"How so?"

"The disappearance of Mary Benton is not well-known; most people have an inkling somebody went missing in a blizzard, but that's about the extent of their knowledge."

"What's your take?"

"There was an old woman, a recluse, who almost certainly is dead now. She lived on a small piece of land outside of the city limits. Once a month, she hired a car to bring her into town for supplies. Nobody knew anything about her; she kept to herself. One day she stopped coming. When people noticed, the police sent a car to the property. There was no sign she had ever lived there, no furnishings, no belongings, the home was empty. I believe the Ice Lady story is a combination of the woman and the vague story of Mary vanishing in the blizzard."

Joel opened the picture from Williams's room on his phone and showed it to Sorenson.

"You ever see this picture before?"

Sorenson shook his head no, "I recognize the Chief, who's the other guy?"

"Charles Patterson, he worked for the railroad."

"Where did you find it?"

"On William's nightstand, I figure it must have some significance for him to display it like a family photograph." Joel didn't mention the piece of lace.

"I've heard old-timers talk disparagingly about the chief." Said Sorenson. "I think there was a hint of scandal around him or at least some bad optics when it came to his associates. Supposedly he aligned himself with unscrupulous moneyed, people. I don't think anything came of it, though."

"I found something interesting in Mary's police file," Joel said. "Somebody tried to file a report three days after her disappearance. According to the entry, the witness was deemed unreliable, and nothing further was recorded in the file."

"You think it was Williams?

Joel shrugged.

"Maybe they didn't like what the person had to say," said Sorenson.

"Maybe."

"What do you know about Patterson?" asked Sorenson.

"His main residence was in Minneapolis, the house in this picture; was a second home built on Shoreline drive. I have a friend in the cities looking at his public records to see what kind of paper trail he left behind."

"Seven Lakes exported a lot of ice," said Sorenson, " if Patterson worked for the railroad, he undoubtedly had involvement with the Ice Works. The company owned a pretty good swath of land fronting the lake. The land along the shoreline was converted into residential lots years ago, but a couple of the original buildings from the operation still exist in the warehouse district."

"What type of buildings?"

"One is the actual Ice House, used to store ice for the local population. Numerous companies have owned it since the 70s. I believe It's vacant now. The original company office building is there; it's just a shell after being vandalized over the years."

"It's not secured?"

"The city put up fencing, even had some barbed wire, but you know how that goes, a kid with a bolt cutter can make short work of chain link, especially if he is looking for a remote place to fool around with his girlfriend or do some underage drinking with his buddies."

"Are those the warehouses referenced by the boys?"

"Yes."

"So, the boy's location would have been within the old ice field?"

"More than likely, is that important?" Sorenson asked, sensing Joel was on to something.

"Could be, hey listen, you have been a huge help, and I cannot thank you enough for taking the time to meet with me." Said Joel,

"Not at all; how about you doing me a favor, and keep me in the loop? Said Sorenson, "I have a feeling you are sitting on an awesome story."

"The story is yours to write," Joel said as he started back toward the entrance.

Joel saw a text from Marty as he crossed the parking lot that said, "Call me." Joel tapped the phone icon under his name.

"Hey, Marty," Joel said when he answered.

"How is it going in Seven lakes? Found the girl yet?"

"Not yet," Joel said, smiling. "I am hot on her trail, though."

"Good." Said Marty, "You might want to add this to your notes."

"What do you have?"

"I was researching railroad archives from the period in question and found a directory of sorts listing people in varying positions who worked for the company. It looks like they published it for internal use."

"Was Patterson in it?"

"Yeah, two listings."

"His two homes?"

"No, his home in Minneapolis and The Seven Lakes Ice Works."

"Interesting, so he had an office on the site of the Ice Works operation, how convenient."

"I am still looking at public records; I think Patterson was a private guy though; there is not much about him, for somebody with his kind of wealth."

"Thank you, Marty, I don't know what I would do without your help."

"You wouldn't solve many cases," Marty said, laughing. "Be careful."

"Will do," Joel replied and said, "goodbye."

CHAPTER 12

(December 21, 1925)

Charles Patterson was in a bad mood when arriving with his wife two hours after the party at the Seven Lakes Grand Hotel was underway. He almost decided not to waste his time; he had a low threshold for socializing with people he believed beneath him. Even though Patterson owned an estate on shoreline drive, it was not his real home; Patterson was not from here. His mood, however, dramatically improved when he spotted a young woman sitting alone near the fireplace.

Patterson, taken aback by her youthful beauty, encouraged his wife to mingle, and she gladly wandered off, feeling fortunate to avoid his condescending narrative. Marriage for Patterson was a front that provided a level of respectability that masked his real interests of vice and debauchery.

Finding a place near the main staircase, Patterson observed the woman from a discreet distance. He sensed an uneasiness in her manner as she feigned happiness for the people around her. Her face lighting up with a smile when anyone approached her, and she eagerly engaged in conversation, but her eyes turned distant, and her expression of worry when the person moved on.

Patterson, struggling, to take his eyes off her, thought it strange that a woman with her looks, was unaccompanied.

Throughout the evening, he made discreet inquiries about her and, being a master of manipulation, subtly set people up to gain the information he sought. His targets, unaware of his intentions, volunteered information freely. He learned she had been staying at the hotel for nearly two weeks, had arrived alone, and, as far as anyone knew, had lived alone the whole time. His instinct said she was desperate, maybe divorced, maybe in trouble with the law. Desperation was useful, especially when he turned it to his advantage.

Patterson had not been careful during his observation, though, and with a room full of people, he had failed to see an older woman watching his preoccupation with the young woman. The woman considering herself a stand-up citizen felt it was her obligation to alert wives of the wayward activities of their husbands.

When the ice sculptor began his carving demonstration, people in the room, including the young woman, formed a semi-circle around the table that held the block of clear ice. Patterson, seeing an opportunity to get closer to the young woman, took up a position slightly behind and to her right. When more guests arrived, the group pressed in to accommodate them, and Patterson moving forward now stood directly to her right. Her perfume in this proximity was intoxicating and fueled his desire. Patterson, a decisive person, knew at that moment, he would have to find a way to gain her company.

CHAPTER 13

(Present)

Joel was fascinated with the endless encounters, interactions, and consequences of people's actions or inactions. If something went wrong, a person went missing or became a victim of murder. Usually, their decisions or indecisions contributed in some way to that result.

Fairview, a town about 45 miles to the west, is where Mary boarded a train for Seven Lakes in December of 1925. Nearly three weeks later, she vanished without a trace.

Tim Bell, the curator of the Fairview Train and History Museum, had been helpful earlier on the phone, and Joel decided it would be worth a trip to see what he could uncover. Joel figured he could find out if Mary's former life had any connection to Fairview.

Joel had assembled an odd list of characters during his initial investigation but didn't know if any of them intersected with Mary. The blizzard of 1925 had been a devasting event, and the official explanation of Mary being caught unaware of its danger, and ill-prepared for its wrath, seemed plausible on the surface. However, it didn't explain the strange letter from a dying man.

The bright sunlight today held no warmth, and heating systems in Fairview struggled to keep the deep freeze from invading warm interiors. When Joel drove through downtown Fairview, he noticed people outside wore expressions of wanting to be somewhere else.

Tim Bell swung the metal museum door open and ushered Joel inside into a cavernous hallway. The man's appearance did not match Joel's impression of him from their phone conversation. Joel pictured an aging boomer with worn jeans and long hair. Bell turned out to be a well-dressed man in his early forties with short hair and a genuine smile that gave Joel the impression that Bell was glad he came.

The main hallway was enormous, and its arched ceiling soared to nearly 20 feet. The sound of the bolt sliding back into place as Bell re-locked the door echoed in the space.

Just a few feet from the entrance, Bell ushered Joel into a comfortable office, sat down behind his desk, and motioned him to sit in one of two leather chairs facing his desk. Joel had explained on the phone the timeframe he was interested in and now went into more detail about Mary's disappearance. He told Bell what he had uncovered so-far, and Bell, fascinated with the story, said, "I feel sad for the young woman if she did perish in the storm. I cannot imagine the horror of being lost in a blizzard in an unfamiliar place." Joel nodded his agreement.

"I need to know who she was, where she came from, what type of life she lived before coming to Seven Lakes. The only thing I know about her past is that she traveled by train to Seven Lakes from Fairview." Joel said.

"That's not much." Bell agreed. Bell, thinking for a moment, said, "If she wasn't from here, we should be able to make logical inferences of where her journey might have started, especially if we know the time and day she arrived into Seven Lakes, it could narrow the search. Logbooks were pretty meticulously maintained, and if they are still in existence, we should be able to trace her backward."

Bell looked up at an ornamental clock extending out from the wall above his door. "My archivist, Ms. Allison, will be arriving shortly. I will see if she can set aside some time to help in your search. She's practically a magician in finding obscure information. I need to take care of a few things before we open the museum to the public. If you don't mind, I will check in on you a little later."

"Not at all," Joel replied.

Ms. Allison arrived ten minutes later, as promised. She was a pretty girl who looked to be in her late twenties or early thirties with short black hair pulled into a bun. She wore unadorned black-framed glasses that gave her an academic appearance. Spotting Joel standing near the entrance of the research room, she hurried down the hallway to introduce herself. Bell had given her a heads up by text or email because she knew his name. Her winter jacket was one of those puffy types with horizontal sections that make the wearer look a bit like the Michelin Man.

Ms. Allison insisted Joel call her Sam as she searched for her key on a ring that looked a little too crowded.

"Alright, Sam, show me to the past," Joel said.

She smiled at this as she turned the key and pushed open the double doors into the research room. Joel following her into the dark space, was amazed at the room's size when she had turned on a series of light switches. The room had the same high ceilings as the hallway, but its walls were covered in bookshelves stretching two-thirds of the way toward the ceiling. There were wooden ladders positioned along each wall attached to metal rails. The only furniture in the room were several high tables with their stools pushed underneath, and a desk covered with varying size stacks of papers.

Sam went to her desk, just a short distance beyond the tables, and slipped out of her jacket while simultaneously looking at some of the paperwork and materials left from her previous day's work. She was a petite woman dressed in a simple dark blue skirt, a white button-down blouse, and flat comfortable looking shoes. Joel thought Sam looked more like a student than a professional archivist. After a few minutes of searching through materials, she wrote a few notes into a journal-style book lying open on her desk before walking over to where Joel was waiting.

"So, Joel, what kind of information are you interested in?"

"I am trying to establish any connection to a woman who disappeared in Seven Lakes in 1925. She arrived into Seven Lakes by train from Fairview, but I don't know if she was from here."

Sam paused for a few seconds said, "I think we should start our search in Fairview, we can use the process of elimination; if we strikeout, then we can always expand out."

"Perfect," said Joel.

Sam went back to her desk and touched a key on her flat keyboard that looked to be the thickness of a few sheets of paper. A large monitor came to life, displaying an expansive landscape with a small box for inputting her password. Sam, not bothering to sit, leaned over the back of her chair to key in the code, and when her desktop appeared, quickly opened an application for searching the internal archives. Joel watched as she studied each result briefly before repeating the process. Moving closer to her desk, he found his eyes were not up to the challenge of reading the small print on her screen. He was impressed with the swiftness of her searches and could see she was adept at her job. After a few additional queries, Sam noticed Joel, and looking up from the screen said, "I have some items to get you started, do you know how old she was?"

For Joel, the question illustrated how much he didn't know about Mary. "I don't know her actual age, just witness accounts that described her as young."

Sam looking at him with a questioning expression, decided to use her judgment. "School rolls are a great place to start. Fairview only had one high school in 1925. If she was from here, she should show up in the yearbooks." Sam said.

Sam looked back at her monitor, her fingers flying across the keys in fits and starts before pausing to scribble numbers onto a post-it note. When finished, she grabbed the sticky-note and headed across the room. Joel went back to the research tables, removed his laptop and notebook, and waited for her to return.

Sam brought a stack of yearbooks covering the date range of 1915 to 1925 and set them on the corner of the table next to Joel. "See if you can find her in these, I have some other property records and directories I will search on my computer," Sam said, returning to her desk, this time settling into her chair.

The morning stretched into the afternoon, and their research turned out to be productive in that they were able to conclude Mary likely never lived in Fairview. Joel had found a kindred spirit in Sam, her enthusiasm and deductive reasoning aligned with excellent investigative techniques.

Once they determined she was not a local, they shifted their focus to the railroad logbooks. "It is not as easy as it might sound," Sam warned, "the possibilities cover dozens of connections into Fairview from a main-line that snakes thousands of miles to the west, east to Duluth and with dozens of north/south branches along the way. To Joel, the map of the railroad in 1925 looked like a malnourished tree lying on its side. Another consideration is whether she spent the night or maybe longer in Fairview, or had she made her connection the same day?

Around 3:00 pm, Joel peered over the top edge of the logbook he was searching and looking across at Sam, saw she was in the same position as the last time he checked. She was sitting in front of her screen, scanning text scrolling at a high rate of speed. Joel was interested in her opinion about Mary; Sam was engaged and possessed a thorough knowledge of the history of the region. She might also have insights about Mary's possible motivations from a female perspective.

He thought about asking her to dinner to thank her for her help, but, in truth, wanted to spend more time in her company. The alternative, driving back to Seven Lakes on a bleak December evening to spend time alone in his hotel room, was a distant second choice. He was hesitant to ask, there was a significant age difference, and the last thing he wanted to do was create an awkward moment with no way for a graceful retreat.

Making up his mind, Joel quietly slid his chair back, stood up, stretched his legs, and casually walked over to her desk. Her cantilever lamp adjusted low; its white light focused on her keyboard. Sam leaned in close to her screen, the side of her face bathed in the white light from the lamp. Sensing movement, she caught him off guard when she turned her head and smiled. Joel, trying to keep the moment light, and allow her plenty of room to opt-out, said, "I got so involved in research, I forgot about sustenance. I was thinking about getting dinner here in Fairview before heading back, would you have time to join me?" The question sounded a bit rehearsed when hearing it out loud, and he instantly regretted having asked. Sam's smile widened, and she replied: "eating is one of my favorite things to do, but I am not sure an underpaid detective can afford to feed me." There was something mischievous in her smile like she knew he was uncomfortable with sticking his neck out.

"I would be willing to try."

Sam, still smiling, said, "In that case, I will have dinner with you, besides I need to talk to you about the case."

Joel felt his anxiety diminish and was relieved the moment had not turned awkward.

"There is a steakhouse about a mile from here, close-in to downtown, it has a low key atmosphere, and the steaks are crazy good. Plus, I have some information I think you will find interesting," Joel was excited at the prospect of new information or any connection she may have uncovered about Mary.

Twenty minutes later, after wrapping up their research, they were seated at a small round table covered with a crisp white tablecloth. The décor of the steakhouse reminded Joel of a Victorian billiards room or library, all dark wood, low light, and cozy nooks for privacy. It was still a bit early for dinner, so they had the place mostly to themselves. Sam explained the after-work crowd wouldn't filter in until around 5:30.

There was a small lamp on their table with a black fringe shade, and the diffused light was complementary to Sam's youthful complexion. When she removed her glasses, Joel noticed how pretty her brown eyes were. A waiter took their drink order before disappearing around the corner of an intricately carved wooden bar that held a remarkable array of bottles lighted from underneath, their colors and shades each promising an escape from the world and its problems.

Sam put her elbows on the table, cradled her face with her hands, and, looking across at Joel, wore the same mischievous smile from earlier at the museum.

"I saw you were checking me out today, while I was hard at work doing research, you were researching me." She said, still smiling. Joel feeling his face turning red, held his hands up like a teller in a bank robbery, and said, "Guilty as charged," before stumbling through an awkward apology. He then added, "You are such a bright, enthusiastic person. I have thoroughly enjoyed working with you today."

"Relax," Sam said, still grinning. "I am giving you a hard time. Would you like to hear what I found online?" Joel exhaled when he realized he had been subconsciously holding his breath and sat back in his chair. He watched her expression turn from mischief to one more serious.

"Have you found a connection to Mary?"

Sam leaned in toward the table, and Joel sensed her excitement as she started to relay what she had found.

"I did some random Googling around using Mary Benton in about a dozen towns on the main-line or one of its branches. I concentrated on a 200-mile circumference using Fairview as the center." Joel nodded that he was following. "I got a hit, not on Mary Benton, but a Christine Benton." Joel looked confused but didn't interrupt.

"Just wait," Sam said, "it gets better. There is a town by the name of Skyland, just south of the Canadian border that sits on a huge lake. It looks like a pretty little town, judging from the online pictures. It is built on a steep incline rising from the shore." Joel was unsure where the story was going, but could easily imagine the town she described.

"So after some more digging," Sam continued, "I found an article dated August 17th, 1920. Check this out." Sam said as her voice gained momentum. She looked down at her phone and fiddled with the keys for a few seconds looking for the screenshot she had sent to herself earlier. Finding it, she read it aloud.

"On the morning of August 16th, the badly bruised body of a naked woman washed ashore just to the east of the town of Skyland. The authorities have been unable to identify her, and they suspect foul play in her death." Sam paused, looking across at Joel; his expression indicated he was intently listening Sam continued, "Two days later, an article published in the same paper had additional details about the unidentified woman." Sam read the article.

On August 18th, the manager of the Clearview hotel in Skyland reported to police that a mother and daughter had checked into the hotel two days earlier on August 16th. The daughter showed up at the front desk on the day after the discovery of the body to report her mother had not returned after leaving for an unknown destination two nights previously. Authorities obtained a positive ID from the girl that the body found on the rocks was her mother."

Joel winced at the thought of the young girl having to ID her mother under those conditions. The quaint town of Skyland had turned dark and foreboding in his mind. He was silent for a moment before, asking, "How old was the daughter?"

"She was 13," Sam said, looking inquiringly at Joel. Joel's mind raced, the age was right, the timeframe was right, the location made sense, the violent end to her mother, her only apparent support system, would have been devastating. She probably never had a chance, he thought to himself.

Sam said, "According to a follow-up article, authorities conducted multiple interviews with the girl and concluded her mother was most likely a traveling prostitute. They suspect a probable motive in her death to be entanglement with a prior client. The daughter, pending location of family or relatives, would likely be sent to the state-run school for orphans in the southern part of the state.

Joel could see the girl's plight had moved Sam emotionally. It was not uncommon in his line of work for investigators to form bonds with voiceless victims in need of advocates. As Joel looked across at Sam, he knew Mary had gained a bright, passionate person willing to fight on her behalf.

"I don't know what happened to Mary in Seven Lakes, but my gut tells me she became a victim of her circumstance." Said Joel.

"How do you mean?"

"I mean, she was young and inexperienced, and her naivety could be what got her into trouble."

Sam, silent for a few minutes, was lost in thought as she tried to imagine the challenges Mary might have faced as a young woman alone in a strange town.

"I forgot to tell you about the dream I had on the night I arrived," Joel said, interrupting her thoughts.

"What was it about?" asked Sam.

"I had been exploring Main Street and ended up at the corner of Main and Shoreline Drive, looking across at the hotel. The scene triggered my memory of the dream from the previous night." Joel paused, trying to recall the scene. "A woman was standing a fair distance from me; everything around her was white; she seemed to be gazing in my direction. I am not sure; she was too far away to tell.

"Did she say anything?"

"No, I am not even sure if she knew I was there. There was something familiar about the location; I had a feeling of déjà vu standing on the corner. In the dream, she started to fade from view; it became harder and harder to see her until finally, she was gone."

"Was she moving away from you?"

"No, the veils became less transparent, and the light dimmer, and she faded out behind them. The worst part was an overwhelming feeling of helplessness I felt when she was gone."

"Have you ever had a dream like that before?"

"No, not like that."

Sam's expression changed to one of sadness and concern. "Joel," she finally said, "It might not be a random coincidence that you are here. You have a connection to this place and its past."

"You might be right," Joel said, remembering how the old letter looked lying on the floor of his Minneapolis office.

CHAPTER 14

(December 22, 1925.)

Patterson, sitting at his desk, was unable to concentrate on the paperwork lying in front of him. His mind preoccupied with the young woman from the previous night's party. Patterson believed his intellect far superior to most people, and he had a knack for obtaining the things he desired. It was unusual for him to be intimidated, but he had the feeling that somehow this woman was out of his reach.

In his travels, he was proficient at sampling the pleasures of local women, despite being short in stature and sporting a waist that had doubled since his twenties. Being overweight had given him an unhealthy pallor. His facial features and skin had a puffiness that, in turn, caused his eyes and lips to look sunken. There was no possibility of anyone mistaking him for handsome. In his favor, though, he possessed a commanding voice and bigger than life presence which people associated with authority.

He had discovered having money went a long way in making up for what one might lack in build or looks. The women he slept with were prostitutes for all intents and purposes who pretended to be his lovers and who he generously supported between visits for the performance. Somewhere in the recesses of his mind, he knew the real score; it was just more palatable for his ego to imagine them as girlfriends awaiting his return.

Being faithful was never a goal or concern for Patterson, working hard, and making money were the essential parts of life. His father, a notorious womanizer, had taught him well about the ways of the opposite sex. Unfortunately, his father had not followed through with the money part, and his family became destitute when Patterson was just a boy.

Marriage for Patterson did not impede multiple partners; it was an arrangement in which he maintained appearances and respectability to satisfy perceived societal expectations. He no-longer entertained relations with his wife and could barely remember a time when he had. Her services to him were more akin to hired help, like running the household in his absence, which was often.

He did, however, believe in discretion and maintained his vices, money matters, and business dealings close to the vest, confiding in no one.

His desire for the young woman grew progressively worse as the day wore on, turning into a full-blown obsession. The longer he thought about her, the worse it became. He had undressed her in his mind a dozen times while scheming to arrange a meeting. It was one thing in his travels, to bed professional working women in towns hundreds of miles from anywhere, but here in Seven Lakes, he was a homeowner. And he needed the benefits derived from that particular level of respectability. No, here, he would need to exercise caution.

He was in too deep to turn back or summon the willpower of a more reasonable self. His desire had moved beyond rational thought, and any reason not to pursue this particular longing, degraded into internal arguments, he could no longer win.

Pushing the paperwork aside, he opened his top desk drawer and pulling out a piece of blank stationery, placed it on the desk. He decided to invite Mary here, to his office tonight. He knew he couldn't take a chance of being seen in town with her, but if she could manage to find her way here, there was virtually zero chance of an association with him. He didn't use the office often, and to say it was off the beaten path was an understatement. It was close to a mile to the hotel with little in the way of civilization in-between. He knew it was a long-shot, and her willingness to come would depend on whether his hunch about her desperation is accurate.

As he wrote the note, he made the time of the proposed meeting well after working hours. He left the reason ambiguous to elicit Mary's interpretation of the invite. If she had financial difficulties, she might see it as an opportunity.

He would have to somehow deliver the note without raising suspicion within the corps of hotel employees who were notorious for loose gossip. He was unsure of how he might accomplish the task but too impatient to worry with those minor details now. Regardless, once she had the invitation, if his assumptions proved right, he would soon have his answers.

He wrote the simple note in a cursive style, folded it, and stuffed it into an envelope. He printed "Mary" in small letters across the front and would add a room number later if and when he obtained it. Leaning back in his chair, Patterson closed his eyes, trying to recreate the scene from the party when standing by her side, and breathing in her perfume. He could see her smile, her contemplative stares, and reactive expressions. Each scene he imagined framed in soft light where she was the only person in focus.

CHAPTER 15

(December 22, 1925.)

Weather reporting in 1925 was still somewhat of an inexact science. Two developing systems, one moving north from the Gulf of Mexico and one sliding south out of Canada, had been on a collision course for several days. Where precisely the two would meet, and what would be the result, was the tricky part.

Mrs. Patterson had grown up as Lucy Hanson in a family of two children. Her parents, poor homestead farmers, had tried to eke out a living on the prairies of Minnesota, where inhospitable weather was part of life. Most of her childhood, she spent trying to survive. Her older brother, by two years, didn't survive; he died in the winter of Lucy's fifth year. Her family rarely had enough money for even basics, and they suffered from inadequate food supplies regularly. Lucy's mother died when she was 16, and when Lucy turned 18, she left the farm and its meager existence behind, traveling to the cities to look for work. A year later, her father died, and Lucy was all alone in the world.

She met Charles Patterson while working as a waitress in a St.Paul diner. Patterson, who was socially awkward, started visiting her regularly. In the early days, he was an insurance salesman who seemed to do pretty well for himself. Patterson, when drinking, would follow her home and spend the night in her tiny apartment. She was surprised the day he asked her to marry him. Lucy knew she was not in love with him, but desperately wanted the financial security he could provide. She was all too familiar with the misery of poverty and determined she would never return to that type of life.

The night of the Christmas celebration at the Seven Lakes Grand hotel, an older woman who Lucy had never met approached her in the dining room. The woman introduced herself as Mildred of McClellan farms as if Lucy should know the place. Mildred, unsolicited, told her how she observed Lucy's husband's with more than a slight interest in a young woman. The woman in question was somebody who had a room at the hotel. The overtones of Mildred's narrative layered with innuendo left little doubt of her opinion on the matter. Lucy suspected Mildred, who was still rattling on, enjoyed her role as informant a bit too much. "Nobody knows anything about her, other than she arrived by train a couple of weeks ago, and she has been staying here ever since," Mildred said with bitterness. Lucy, having heard enough and concerned about the people around her, who pretended not to be listening, abruptly ended the one-sided conversation with Mildred.

"Don't say I didn't warn you," Mildred said, retreating from an agitated Lucy, who looked like she was about to hurt the messenger.

Lucy did, however, understand the problem; she could not allow her husband to play her for a fool. For better or worse, she was now a part of Seven Lakes. Unlike her husband, who felt superior to most people, Lucy knew her place was a closer match to the intellect and commonness of the locals. Her elevation in status was purely financial, and 100 percent attributable to her husband. If her husband had romantic intentions toward a young woman, Lucy would need to insert herself into his path.

Her husband planned to stay in Seven Lakes through the holidays and then return to the cities. Which meant she only had a few days to get through before she could leave Seven Lakes behind. It was not about faithfulness; she had no illusions that her husband was faithful; he had lost interest in her shortly after marriage. It was about risk, the risk of losing her lifestyle, and the status that came with it. She was not about to give that up to a young hussy who her husband couldn't see the danger she posed.

The morning after the party, Lucy watched her husband leave for his office at the Ice Works. He was grumbling as he left, and when the door shut, the sound of his voice trapped outside returned the interior of the house to silence. Lucy watched him cross the expansive frozen lawn, a fog of condensation around his head as he exhaled into the frigid air. The grass was flat and depressing yellow-brown color, and at that moment, she longed for warmer temperatures, and the soft Minnesota grass she used to lie in as a little girl watching billowy white clouds against a blue sky on a summer afternoon.

Standing alone in the empty house, devoid of a housekeeper, she replayed the conversation with Mildred. She had never invaded her husband's privacy before; there was an implied rule that his study was off-limits whether he was home or not. He had built the same office in Seven Lakes as was in their Minneapolis home. Bookshelves covered the wall behind his desk, and the books with luxurious leather bindings populated the shelves. The books were strictly decorative, though; the pages blank. It gave the space an academic look based on a lie. She wondered as she approached the study door, what other lies the room might hold. The glass doorknob was cold to her touch, and when she turned it, she felt the spring-loaded latch slide within its casing. There was a whoosh of air as she forced the door open slightly, and when she released the knob, the door swung inward several inches on its own accord. Lucy sliding through the opening shivered slightly from nerves. Her instinct told her to retreat, but she stood her ground, not willing to concede just yet.

After standing in the room for several seconds, she turned and pushed the door closed, shutting herself inside the study. She could smell the pungent odor of cigars, an earthy smell she did not find unpleasant. The dark wood of his desk and shelves, heavy curtains, and the deep reds of the Oriental rug gave the room a cozy masculine feel even though it was quite a sizable space.

Her husband's massive desk, evenly spaced between the walls, was set back from the entrance, leaving a partially open floor space filled by two chairs and a couch set into a conversational style grouping. She found the furniture ironic because she couldn't remember a time anyone had ever visited their Minneapolis home and was pretty sure no one would ever visit here either. She also was not welcome in his office, so she wondered who her husband planned to have conversations with — another lie of perception, perhaps.

There were only a few pieces of paper on his desk, and upon closer inspection, she saw they were invoices associated with construction expenses. Lucy had no idea of what her husband's financial situation might be and was never involved in any decisions concerning money. He did not even tell her about building the Seven Lakes home until construction was well underway. When he did mention it, it was just to let her know that if it finished on-time, he planned to spend the Christmas holidays there.

The windows of the office overlooked the front-drive and the frozen lake beyond. The Iron Gate at the end of the drive opened onto shoreline drive. It was an impressive view from where the house stood, setback on a slightly higher elevation of the land. Sitting at his desk, he could observe his kingdom. The long gravel drive straight up from the Gate made a full circle in front of the house. A fountain with no water stood in a grassy area that the drive encircled. It was probably for the best; it would be a solid block of ice now. She moved slowly around his desk, careful not to touch anything. When she reached his chair, she rolled it back slightly, making a mental note to put the wheels back into the indentations of the oriental rug. Sitting down in his chair, she pulled back on two ornate knobs attached to the center drawer. The drawer moved a fraction of an inch before catching on a locking mechanism. She had the same results with the three drawers on the right side of the desk, each moving slightly before catching and holding.

Lucy leaned back in his chair and studied the keyhole in the center drawer before looking around at the infinite places a key might be hidden in the office. She did not think it unusual the desk was locked; it was her increased wariness that had brought her into his private realm in the first place. Lucy had no idea what to look for or what to do if she found something; she had not thought that far ahead. She just felt a need to know what she was dealing with, and that need drove her uncharacteristic behavior.

If she could observe her husband in the room, he might unintentionally give up the key's location. While this sounded logical on the surface, Lucy was sure she did not dare to carry it off and cringed at the thought of being caught spying. Besides, the key might not be in the room at all; maybe he carried it with him.

The one advantage she did have, was that her husband was a creature of habit, and whatever his routine or wherever the key was, it would always there. She thought about the prospect of concealing herself in the room and immediately dismissed the idea as too dangerous. Standing up, she moved the chair back into the original indentations and went out into the main hall, closed the door, and getting down on her knees, peered through the keyhole. The narrow field of vision included a partial view of his desk. It was not perfect, but less risky than being in the room. The problem would be in trying to keep track of him if he was not in her field of vision. Leaning back from the keyhole, she looked down the hallway for an escape route if he were to come toward the door suddenly. The entrance to the formal dining room was less than 10 feet from her location and would be the only place to disappear quickly.

Standing up, she reentered the study and walking to the window; enjoyed a view she had not realized existed. She could feel cold radiating through the glass as she stood close to the panes. The day from her vantage point looked lovely, and as she looked across the ice of Seven Lakes, she saw a bank of clouds barely visible forming on the northern horizon.

CHAPTER 16

(Present)

Joel looked across the table at Sam as they sat in a small breakfast café in Fairview. He couldn't imagine anywhere else in the world he would rather be. It was hard to explain how alive he felt when he was around her and knew emotionally; he was in the deep end of the pool. He was terrified to think something that felt so right could quickly turn out not to be a thing.

They had agreed to meet for breakfast the day before when Sam called to tell him she had discovered valuable information about Mary's stay at the State School. As it turned out, she was only in the institution less than a month before being put into a foster home—the home, in the small town of Still Creek, less than 50 miles from Fairview. Mary was of an age where she could be a productive worker and helpful to a family. There was a good chance the family who took her in, learned about her plight from newspaper reports of her mother's death.

Sam was wearing her serious expression this morning, one he had seen before in the museum when she helped with the original search into Mary's past. She looked younger today; maybe it was the way she wore her hair, he was still acutely aware of their age difference.

"Are you OK? Joel asked.

"Yeah, I am fine," Sam replied, still looking serious. She looked into his eyes for a moment and then lowering her voice said, "Do you think there is any connection between your dreams and Mary's disappearance?" Joel shifted in his chair, it was an odd question, and he was unsure how to answer. He probably should not have confided in her about what had turned into a recurring dream of the same woman.

"I don't know, the dreams did start after arriving in Seven Lakes, but I wouldn't want to assume they are connected, they're just dreams."

A waitress appeared, and they stopped their conversation until she took their order and disappeared into the kitchen. Sam, quiet for a minute, finally said, "You know there have been problems at that hotel in the past?" That was something Joel wasn't expecting to hear.

"What do you mean, what kind of problems?"

"There is an odd story from when they renovated it in the '90s. I couldn't remember the details, so I looked it up this morning before you arrived."

"Of course you did." Sam made a face.

"Sorry, I didn't mean to interrupt, continue."

"The hotel was vacant for nearly twenty years after it closed in the '70s. It had extensive damage from neglect and transients who broke in during inclement weather. The renovation involved a complete tear-out, down to the studs. When the workman demolished the fourth floor, they found a sealed room."

"Sealed?" Joel said, raising his eyebrows.

"Yeah, walled over, doors, windows, like the room never existed, like they wanted it to disappear," Joel couldn't imagine what could motivate an owner or manager to take such drastic action.

"According to one of the construction workers, the room had all of its furniture, and the bed made up. The worker said that except for decades of dust, the room looked like it was ready to host its next guest."

"Any idea when it was closed it up?"

"They figured, sometime in the thirties, based on subsequent upgrades in the rest of the hotel."

"Why would a hotel seal up a room?" Joel asked to no one in particular.

"My guess," Sam said slowly, "the employees refused to go in, or guests reported seeing things. It would have been ruinous to have those stories circulating."

"Have you ever seen any reporting like that about the hotel?"

"No, if something was going on, the hotel kept it under wraps. I imagine in those days, it would have been common to threaten an employee's livelihood if found spreading rumors."

Sam reaching across the table, placed her hands on top of Joel's. The smooth warmth of her touch was unexpected, and he saw concern in her eyes. "Why don't we drive up to Still Creek today? I can call the museum, request a personal day. It will give us a chance to see where Mary lived after her mother died." Sam said, her voice trailing off. "Deal," Joel said without hesitation.

An hour later, Joel eased the Bel Air onto a two-lane highway heading north. The deserted road framed between flat frozen plains of farmland stretching to the horizon in both directions. The flatness only interrupted by lonely farmhouses shielded with small stands of trees.

Sam kept up a steady stream of questions and observations about the case as they drove and freely offered ideas on what might have happened to Mary. Some of her questions were more like statements, not meant for answers, more like thinking aloud to gain clarity for herself.

Since the day Joel visited the police department and reviewed Mary's file, he had felt a responsibility to find out what happened to her. Mary was a real person who had hopes and dreams like everyone else. He believed she had suffered an injustice that ended her short life and didn't want to consider the possibility that he would not be able to solve her case.

Sam, silent for a few minutes, was fixated on her phone, and intermittently tapped the screen at a rapid rate with her forefinger before looking up to stare at the highway sliding beneath them.

"Do you believe someone murdered Mary?" Sam asked, turning to Joel.

"It's entirely possible." He finally said. "I know there could be other explanations, but the letter from old man Williams seems to imply something nefarious. Then there is the evidence from the police report that mentions a man delivering a note on the same day she went missing. Why did she leave the hotel and venture into a bad storm? What was so important that it couldn't wait until the storm subsided?"

Joel looked over at Sam; saw that she had turned slightly toward her door and was looking out her side window. "On the flip side," he continued, "the argument against foul play is nearly as compelling. I mean, she was a virtual stranger in a small town that I wouldn't consider dangerous. She was living in a hotel surrounded by people. It is hard to imagine someone wanting to harm her intentionally. Of course, we know little of her past; there could have been someone dangerous who followed her to Seven Lakes. My gut is, whatever happened, it was not pre-meditated. But, the fact that she vanished leads me to believe the crime was in the cover-up. Sam, looking thoughtful, nodded her head slightly as if agreeing with his theories.

Joel, changing the subject, asked her about work at the museum.

"I have a large archive project from a prominent Fairview family; there are letters, diaries, and other correspondence to be categorized. It is somewhat of a daunting task from the perspective of figuring out an organizational structure, but for now, I am enjoying reading about how people of means lived in those days."

Joel slowing down, turned right, onto a secondary road that looked like it had not received new asphalt in decades. The road heading in a northwest direction looked even more remote than the deserted highway they had just left. There was less farmland now, replaced with stands of evergreen, birch and assorted hardwoods, the expansive sky over the flatlands, replaced with small patches of blue between treetops.

According to Joel's phone, this stretch of road would eventually dump them into "Still Creek," where Mary spent five years of her young life in a foster home after her mother's death. Joel figured the timing for Mary could not have been much worse. Mary, almost a woman, loses her mother and forced to live with strangers in the middle of nowhere.

Fifteen minutes along the uneven road, the speed limit dropped to 35 MPH right before the town of Still Creek materialized after rounding a curve. Like a lot of rural America, the passage of time had not been kind to Still Creek. An impressive looking building, probably once the town's bank, stood on a prominent corner as you entered, the year 1921 etched into its cornerstone. The ornately decorated building had boarded up windows and stood as testimony to a more prosperous Still Creek. Continuing along the Avenue revealed more shuttered buildings throughout its Main Street. One could easily imagine the town fading into oblivion when its remaining residents died off.

Near the end of the former business district, there were two cars parked in front of a small restaurant. The people inside were the first sign that anyone still inhabited the town. A neon OPEN sign in the front window, missing part of its O, looked like CPEN.

From the small amount of research Joel had done on the town, he knew the railroad had played a role in its prosperity. Lumber, an economic driver, and main export had relied on railroad transport to get their finished product to market. As they drove beyond the former commercial center, they could see old rail equipment randomly parked on abandoned spur lines that ran alongside deteriorating buildings that were probably once active lumber mills. The rusted cars and equipment looked like it hadn't moved in decades, and when everything stopped moving, the town started to die.

The houses were mostly two-story wooden structures with clapboard siding in need of paint. The remaining population had probably aged to a point where maintaining a home was no longer an option.

Sam, quiet as they surveyed the town, turned to Joel and said, "It is quite a sad little place, isn't it?" She was thinking about Mary and how traumatic it would have been to lose her mother and then forced to assimilate into a strange town.

Joel spotting the street sign he had been looking for just beyond a warehouse built too close to the road, turned onto the lane that would take them to the foster home where Mary lived after her mother's death.

Residential homes, in need of repair, lined the narrow street for a block or so before vegetation started to occupy both sides of the lane. In essence, the road curving to the right continued to narrow as gray leafless branches and vines encroached. Joel spotting an abandoned two-story on the left, that sat on a small rise, slowed down. The house, set back from the road a fair distance, had a wooden picket fence and gate leaning precariously forward as if at any moment it might topple over.

Seeing the house, and knowing Mary once lived there, gave Joel the same feeling he experienced at the police station looking at her list of possessions. Mary was a real person with a real-life, and this house represented another tangible connection to her.

Stopping the car in the middle of the lane, Joel got out to look at the overgrown drive leading up to the front of the home. Deciding it would be better not to try to navigate the Bel Air through the overgrowth. He opened the driver's side door and sticking his head in said: "It looks like we need to walk from here." Sam buttoning up her jacket, pulled on the wool mittens that she put on top of a heat vent, and now were toasty warm.

Starting up the drive together, Joel took the lead and cleared a path through the vines, which made a loud snapping noise when bent in the opposite direction. There was a slight breeze from the north, and Joel estimated the temperature somewhere in the mid-twenties. The cloudy sky, and diffused light, painted the scene a dreary gray monotone.

Approaching the home, he could see the front porch had once been painted white but now a weathered gray. There were only a few random pieces of tar paper remaining on the steeply pitched roof, and the exposed wood had the same weathered appearance as the porch and clapboards. The front door was slightly ajar, and most of the windows still retained their muntins but were missing glass panes. The porch had caved in rotted floor-boards exposing the frozen ground below along with old beer and soda cans.

Joel stopped before crossing the porch to survey its safety. He thought about Mary and how she might have felt upon arriving on this very spot for the first time. Looking back, Sam was picking her way through dormant underbrush in front of the house. He watched her reach down and pick up a small metal cover.

Sam, as a child, had kept treasures in repurposed metal containers, and she wondered if the lid had been for a similar purpose.

Joel, deciding there was still enough support in the porch floor, made his way across to the door, walking along one of the joists for good measure. The rotting door had sagged until its bottom rested heavily on the porch floorboards, moving it, caused a loud scraping noise as Joel forced it open wider to allow his 6-foot plus frame through. Stepping inside, he tried to imagine people within the space. The emptiness and neglect were trying to erase any notion that it had once been a home. There was an accumulation of dirt on all the floors and vines squeezing between floorboards, spread across wall surfaces, and looked like veins. Nature worked night and day tirelessly to reclaim the land, and this home was well on its way to succumbing to her onslaught.

Joel could barely make out a pattern in the faded wallpaper remaining in a section of the dining room on his left. Directly in front of him, a staircase, missing its handrail, ascended to the second floor. Beyond the stairs, there was opening in the far wall where a fireplace had once stood — the variation in paint color around its opening, indicating its missing mantel.

Despite the freezing temperature inside, Joel felt clammy and a bit claustrophobic. He was keenly aware that Mary once roamed these very rooms, and the fact that she did, somehow made him uncomfortable. He sensed an unseen pressure pushing against him from all sides.

He heard Sam enter through the front door, followed by a low whistle tone indicating her assessment of the scene. Joel, thankful for the distraction, turned back toward her and said, "Welcome home."

Sam smiling walked to the foot of the stairs to look up at the second level.

"We need to make sure they're safe before we go up," Joel said, anticipating her question. Joel walking back to stairs, examined their treads with his hands before putting pressure on them with his foot. He couldn't feel any sponginess, and the water damage appeared to be mostly staining. Joel climbed each step by first placing his partial weight on it before declaring it safe and moving to the next. Sam waited until he was halfway up before she followed.

Joel felt even more claustrophobic as he approached the landing the space feeling small, with the walls pressing in. He hoped Sam wouldn't notice his anxiety level as he wiped beads of sweat from his forehead.

The landing was nearly a perfect square with two hallways running in either direction to the right and left. Joel could see daylight streaming through the ceiling of a bedroom at the end of the hall, and moved slowly through the darker hallway toward the light. He lost track of Sam and was unsure if she had followed him up the stairs. Reaching the bedroom, Joel saw the floor was unsafe from water that had been coming through a gaping hole in the roof. Looking back, he saw Sam standing near the top of the stairs.

"Is the hallway safe?" she called out.

"Yes, it's fine." He replied. He knew she was about to make her way down the hall toward him, and he tried hard to disguise his anxiety. Starting back, he stopped at the entrance to a second bedroom missing its door and noticed a latch like impression on the outer frame.

"Watch your head," Sam said as she approached to stand beside him. Joel looking up, saw a single electrical wire hanging down about a foot from the ceiling. He had not noticed it when passing in the other direction.

The hallway felt suffocating to Joel, and if Sam had not been there, he would have already left the house.

"The room at the end is unsafe." He said, and moving in the direction of the stairs; he saw a bathroom on the right that still had some of its original white octagonal tiles intact around the threshold and perimeter where they extended beneath baseboards. A sizable expanse of the flooring remained beneath the tub, probably because of the herculean effort it would take to remove. The tub, an old claw-foot style, was filthy and full of debris. The plumbing which had once run through the floor was missing, and the holes looked like two dark eyes staring up at him. The room stripped bare except for the tub, gave clues to its layout in unpainted surfaces.

Joel staring into the filthy tub, heard Sam entering the room behind him. He listened to her voice, but it sounded distant and weak, turning to look at her, he hoped she would not notice his apprehension.

"Joel, I was calling your name, and you were not responding, did you hear me?" Joel, unsure, asked, "Just now?"

"Yes, I was right behind you, here in the room, I think you left the scene for a bit, are you feeling OK?" Joel nodded that he was alright and said, "My ears plugged for some reason, and everything sounds muffled." He could see she wasn't buying it.

"Is there something going on, you're not telling me?

Joel hesitating said, "I think there is something about the house, I have had a bad feeling ever since I came inside, I feel like it is closing in on me. "You should have told me." Closing the space between them and taking his hand, she led him from the bathroom, down the stairs, and out the front door. Joel could feel the external pressure ease once he was outside.

Picking their way silently through the underbrush, they tried to stay on the small path Joel forged upon arrival. Once inside the car, Joel started the engine, and heated air instantly flowed from the vents. Sam sliding across the seat into his arms, pressed her petite frame firmly against him. Her hair smelling of exotic spices, he held her tight. After several minutes, Sam looking up said: "You need to promise me you will be careful; there might be things in play we don't understand." Searching his face to see if he understood what she was saying. Joel nodded before leaning forward and pressing his lips against hers while pulling her even closer.

CHAPTER 17

(Present)

Jean Lundquist, a self-appointed historian for Seven Lakes, is the person Beth from the bookstore, told Joel he needed to connect with for anything to do with Seven Lakes past. Jean, a permanent fixture at the Historical Society, helped Joel gather materials from the time of the storm and its aftermath.

The Seven Lakes Historical Society and Museum inhabited an old building a few blocks west of Main Street. It was evident the operation had outgrown its existing building and was not well funded. Fortunately, the helpful staff made up in service for what they lacked in modernization and technology. The information was there; it was just a bit of a manual process to find.

Early newspapers published in Seven Lakes were not digitally archived, and their hard copies still kept in oversized books, arranged by date going back a hundred-plus years.

The research room took up a good portion of the left side of the ground level and had a set of double glass doors at its entrance. There was only one microfiche machine in a small enclosed area in the corner of the room, and its whirring motor advancing film seemed to run continuously.

The room had a substantial research table, and two older gentlemen who are sitting at one end discussed cases involving local crimes and criminals from the past. Joel's name scribbled on a yellow post-it note attached to a folder had been placed on the opposite side of the table.

Taking a seat near the folder, he tore a blank page from his notebook and began sketching a flow-chart diagram. At the top of the page, he placed Williams's name inside a sketch of an envelope. Drawing a line from the envelope to the right, ending in a square, he labeled as a photograph. He then printed the names, Charles Patterson and Gerald Swanson to the right of the square. In parenthesis, he noted Patterson as the owner of the home and put the chief of police beside Swanson's name. In the center of the page, he drew a circle and placed Mary's name inside. He then connected the circle to the envelope. From the left side of the circle, he tied it to another rectangle labeled evidence. He drew a short line from the evidence rectangle down and wrote "unreliable" in parenthesis, he wrote ("possible witness.") He drew a short line from the right of the box and wrote the words ("note delivered to Mary on the day she disappeared.")

Joel studied the drawing for a few minutes before pushing it aside and opening the prepared folder. Most of the papers inside were enlarged copies of newspaper articles from 1925. There were a few near the top with first-hand descriptions of the blizzard. Joel scanned the reports, looking for any mention of Mary. He found a small write-up nearly identical to the one he had read online and concluded the information likely originated in the Seven Lakes Chronicle.

Just like the file on Mary in the basement of the county building, the case in the public domain was short-lived. The official conclusion of death by exposure acceptable under the circumstances, and without a body to prove or disprove it, life in Seven Lakes moved on. Joel turned through the pages, unable to find any additional mention of Mary beyond the original reporting.

Joel noticed a recurring weekly column titled, "Seven Lakes Residents." Reading through several of the columns, he noted that the comings and goings of ordinary residents who ventured to Iowa or the Twin Cities were considered news. He also found a half-page advertisement about an upcoming Christmas celebration at the Seven Lakes Grand hotel, scheduled for the evening of December 21. The ad included a menu in addition to planned entertainment for the evening.

Jean had included an artist rendering of the hotel in the folder; the pencil sketch most likely would have been used in advertising. Seeing the picture reminded him of the magazine ad found among Mary's belongings. The rendering of the hotel was from the perspective of the park across Main Street. The picture showing an elegant wrap-around porch that no longer existed today.

A thought suddenly occurred to Joel that he had not yet considered. Was it possible Mary intended to end her life? Considering it for a moment, he found it problematic because of the lack of supporting evidence. She had not left a note or given any indication that would lead one to that conclusion.

Joel unfolded an area map dated 1900 that Jean had included in the folder. The map showed a small business district mainly concentrated near the shoreline that stretched less than five blocks to the south. With the residential streets running parallel to Main, and the cross streets, the whole area probably only equated to a half square mile. The lakefront, still mostly undeveloped, had a small dirt road that followed the shoreline for about a mile in either direction—the road running to the East ended at the Seven Lakes Ice Works. The Grand Hotel did not exist, and there weren't any homes built along the shoreline road. A traveler taking the lane to the west would have left civilization behind after just a few blocks. On the other side of Main, across from where the hotel eventually would be built, was a park with a pavilion. A railroad spur line forked from the Main and angled northwest through wooded acreage before cutting across the Ice Works property and then merging back into the mainline a mile Beyond.

A later map from the 20s showed the hotel in-place, and a few homes built along the shore. Most of the land was still heavily wooded, and the majority of the lakeshore remained undeveloped.

The older men at the table were still conversing, and Joel overheard one of them talking about a book he had written about early crimes in the region. Joel walking over to where the men sat, introduced himself, and told them about his research on Mary Benton.

"I couldn't help overhear your conversation about your book and was wondering if you wouldn't mind taking a look at an old photograph for me?"

"Sure, where's the photo?" John, the author, asked. Joel placed his phone on the table with the picture displayed between the two men, not wanting to exclude the non-author.

"I don't recognize the fellow on the left, but the man on the right is Gerald Swanson, he was the chief of police from around 1916, to I believe the early '40s," John said.

"Any relation to the current chief?"

"Grandson."

John picked up Joel's phone to look closer, "That house they're standing in front of is one of the earliest mansions built along the waterfront, and I understand there was a bit of mystery surrounding it."

"Oh?" Said Joel.

"Yes, rumor and speculation mostly. Townspeople with active imaginations, I suspect. It sat vacant for a couple of years, and neighbors reported seeing shadows and other movements from inside when it supposedly was closed up. You know how people are, more interesting to believe something sinister than admit a perfectly boring explanation."

Joel nodded in agreement.

"Was it abandoned?"

"I don't think so," John replied, "I understand the person who built it lived in Minneapolis and probably found it inconvenient to live in two homes."

"Do you know about the woman who disappeared in the 1925 snowstorm?" asked Joel.

"I don't have a recollection of that," John paused, "there is a local legend about a woman who appears before storms that they call the "Ice Lady."

"I have heard about that," Joel replied.

"According to the legend, if a person sees her, it is a precursor to severe weather," John said.

"There was an article in your newspaper a couple of days ago about some boys seeing strange lights on the ice. The reporter alluded to the legend in his write-up," said Joel.

"Anything to sell some newspapers, I suppose," John mused.

"The woman who disappeared wasn't from Seven Lakes." Joel said, "I think the hardships the area faced in recovering from the storm, caused her case to fall through the cracks, and people mostly forgot about her; The case had little follow-through after the initial report."

Joel could see Jean through the double doors turning off lights in the main hallway as she was preparing to close up for the day.

John said, "I have a lot of research material I used for putting my book together. You are welcome to any of those materials if you think it would help."

"Thank you," said Joel, "how can I get in touch?"

"If this place is open, I will be in this chair, if not, check the obituary section of the Chronicle," John said with a smile.

Joel laughed, recognizing himself in John's statement of work. "I better gather my stuff before Jean throws us out. I appreciate your help," Joel said, looking at both men even though John's friend had not uttered a word.

It was late when Joel returned to his hotel room; the wind from the lake buffeted the French doors leading to a small balcony. Clutching a steamy mug of coffee in both hands, he stood in front of the doors staring into the blackness. He couldn't see anything beyond the glass but was thankful it shielded the bitterly cold winds off the ice.

Checking email on his phone, he saw one in his inbox from the forensic lab in Minneapolis with an attachment. Tapping the PDF file, he waited for it to open. The report stated simply that the sample fabric's material was made of pure silk and based on its pattern and construction; its estimated manufacture date would be the early 20s.

Goosebumps raised on Joel's arms as he understood the possibility the fabric may have belonged to Mary.

CHAPTER 18

(December 22, 1925)

Patterson made his way into town and enjoyed lunch in the warmth of his favorite eatery on Main Street. He had taken it upon himself to fortify his soft drink with one of the fine corn liquors he kept in a flask. The product produced illegally in the Land of 10,000 Lakes was a desired commodity throughout the region.

The diner, located a couple of short blocks from the hotel, was as decent a place as any to figure out how to deliver the note he had written earlier. As he watched Main Street from a window seat, Patterson half hoped to see the young woman on the street. He had already consumed the equivalent of three shots of the liquor and was feeling a pleasant warmth and contentment. Motioning for the waitress to bring him another Coke, the young woman, aware of his routine, brought one with plenty of room for customization. After finishing his fourth drink, he slipped the waitress a hefty tip before leaving the diner and walking in the direction of the hotel.

He didn't have an actual plan; experience taught him opportunities were often excellent substitutes for plans, and usually offered more flexibility. He was feeling pretty good and, in retrospect, had probably been a bit too generous with the amount of alcohol in preparing his drinks. He had that feeling drinkers get when the world around them is a bit out of sync, and motion and sound operate independently of each other. He had to concentrate on the simple things, like walking straight and keeping his balance.

Approaching the hotel from the opposite side of the street, he saw a flurry of activity in front. Several cars commissioned by the hotel had returned from the rail station and were unloading luggage and passenger's who were in town for the holidays. The scene looked like an opportunity, and he crossed the street and assimilated himself into the fray. When entering the lobby, he saw that the arrivals had practically surrounded the reservation desk waiting to check-in. The hotel staff scurried in every direction, trying to assist.

Patterson positioned himself at the back of the line, acted as if he was waiting his turn to check-in. To the right of the desk check-in counter, luggage piled against a wall looked like a formidable challenge for the bell-hop who busied himself trying to sort it out. Patterson, leaving the line, walked near the bell-hop and said, "Say, son, I have a message for one of your guests from the haberdashery" the bell-hop without looking up nodded to indicate he was listening. Patterson continued, "She is staying here at the hotel," he paused, "Mary," Patterson acted like he was looking for the note. The bell-hop, still looking at the luggage, said: "Mary Benton, in 411." Patterson thanked him and made his way back through the line of people, crossed the lobby, and started up the main staircase. It was a better outcome than he expected and now would not have to rely on hotel staff to deliver the note, where privacy had a good chance of being compromised.

Several minutes later, tired from dragging his weight up the four flights of stairs, Patterson stood outside 411 out of breath. Looking up and down the hallway, he made sure no one was about before pressing his ear against the door. Hearing nothing from inside the room, Patterson slipped the envelope under the door and retreated to the staircase. The trip back down was more comfortable, and when reaching the main floor, he left through the front entrance. As far as he could tell, nobody had paid him any attention.

CHAPTER 19

(Present)

Joel noticed something different about his room when he opened his eyes. He was lying on his side, facing the window, and could barely make out the dark shadowy shapes of the curtains. Bringing his left wrist close to his face, he saw the faint green luminance of his watch hands, indicating it was nearly 7:30 AM. Usually, by now, the light would be leaking around the edges of the window, but today, the room remained dark.

Pushing his legs from under the covers and over the side of the bed, he used their downward motion as leverage to sit up. Grabbing the sheets as they slipped from his upper body, he pulled them back up to wrap around his shoulders. Leaning forward, he placed his forearms above his knees and stayed hunched over until the fog of sleep began to clear.

The air around his exposed feet was colder than he remembered, and a dull ache behind his eyes indicated the barometric pressure had changed during the night.

A cold air mass out of Canada had pushed through the northern and mid-section of the state, and its leading-edge was now sitting just south of Seven Lakes. The low clouds brought in with the front had sucked the color out of everything in town, leaving a grayscale world in its place. The mercury overnight had dropped an additional 10 degrees, making the current mean temperature a frigid 7 degrees Fahrenheit.

Sitting on the edge of the bed, staring into the darkness, he recalled having had a strange dream again. The woman, walking among wispy white curtains of varying transparencies, faded in and out of view, depending on her distance. At one point, she came physically close to him, and when she turned to move away, he saw her features lacked definition from a side profile. It was a jumbled confusing sequence like most dreams, and the images were already retreating into his subconscious.

There is nothing quite like the sensation of stepping from a warm environment into temperatures that barely hover above zero. Joel remembered delivering newspapers as a youth in the dead of winter with his scarf tied across his face, and ice crystals forming within the material from exhaling, the moisture in his breath essentially freezing in mid-air.

As he left the hotel today, it reminded him of those frigid mornings. There still wasn't any significant snowfall in Seven Lakes, but the clouds hovering low this morning had a disagreeable look threatening to change that equation.

When he arrived at the Seven Lakes Public library, he found the Librarian, Mrs. Cantey, sitting at her desk. Canty had assembled materials for Joel based on the information he had provided her earlier. The room was warm and smelled of freshly brewed coffee and books. Joel found a table near the back where he could see the dramatic sky of the cold-front through clear-story windows that ran the entire perimeter of the building.

Joel read the title of a slender journal-style book on the top of the stack; "I remember these things," it was written by a person who lived in Seven Lakes between 1910 & 1940 and undoubtedly it would have the author's impression of the 1925 storm.

"It was not just the volume of snow that fell, but the incredible height of the drifts from the relentless winds," explained Mr. Giles in a

letter written to his sister in Minneapolis. The correspondence was part of a collection of letters published several years after the storm. *"It has been a struggle to do the simplest of chores, and it took better than a day's work to clear a narrow path to the barn."* The letter continued. Joel knew the conditions described were the conditions Mary confronted the night she went missing. It was logical for Joel to assume that Mary, unless completely naïve, would have believed her destination reasonable in the face of the deteriorating conditions. To Joel, that distance by foot meant less than a mile.

Opening the leather satchel he had placed next to his chair, he pulled out a file he had been compiling since arriving in Seven Lakes. Looking through the papers, he found the grid map copied from the Historical Society. The map showed Seven Lakes as it would have been in the '20s. Placing the map on the table, he marked a small x at the location of the hotel and using the distance legend at the bottom, and his pen as a measuring tool approximated a mile out in four directions. He placed an x in each of these positions before drawing arched lines between them. The resulting diagram formed a one-mile circumference around the hotel.

Looking at the circle, he could see there were only two directions that made any sense. Going north onto the lake would have only been an option if she was looking to take her own life. To the west, the road nearly uninhabited quickly gave-way to rural farmland. That left the business district to the south and a few residences and the Ice Works to the east along Shoreline Drive.

Joel assumed she was going to a particular destination, and knew she could have met someone who took her elsewhere. His gut said that was not the case because travel in the storm would have been tricky.

The most logical conclusion was that she went in the direction of the business district. Had her demise been an impulsive or unplanned accident? Or was it something sinister and premeditated? The evidence pointed to the latter if you took into account the note from the unidentified man in the police report.

Sliding the map to the side, he turned his attention back to the letters. He needed a connection, something that tied Mary to someone other than Mr. Williams, who no longer could articulate what he had seen as a child.

Turning the page, he continued reading the letter when the picture on the adjoining page caught his attention. The image was of the Tudor in the framed photo taken from a different angle showing snowdrifts nearly covering the properties wrought iron fencing and entrance gate. The caption below the picture read, "Shoreline Drive buried in the historic blizzard."

He had no idea how Patterson, the owner of the home, may have intersected with old man William's, but he needed to find out. Looking over at Cantey's desk and not seeing her, he walked toward her area until spotting her ducked between shelves straightening reference books. Sensing him nearby, Cantey stood up and asked him how she could help. Joel showed her the picture on his phone of the two men in front of the Tudor. He explained that the person on the left was Gerald Swanson, who had been chief of police in Seven Lakes from around 1916 to sometime in the early 40s, and the person on the right was the owner of the home in the background, a Mr. Charles Patterson.

"I am familiar with the property; a nice family lives there now, Johnston's, I believe. I never heard of Patterson, though, probably no reason I would have." She said.

"See what you can find on Patterson. This picture was on my client's nightstand in the nursing home, and I am trying to find any connection between my client and Patterson." Joel didn't mention the fabric or the strange figure in the upstairs window of the original photograph.

Thirty minutes later, Cantey found a picture and short article from the Seven Lakes Chronicle dated Sept 12, 1924. The article talked about a prominent family from Minneapolis who were moving to Seven Lakes with plans to build a fashionable home on Shoreline Drive. The article mentioned Patterson as working for the railroad. Joel asked her to keep digging; he needed everything she could find about the man. Cantey, sensing her research as integral, went back to work with a new sense of mission.

About an hour later, she returned, this time with three photocopies of newspaper articles. "I found these, nothing about your client, just information about the construction of Patterson's home, his involvement with the Ice Works, and an announcement about a national retail chain planning a store on Main Street." She said.

Joel skimmed the first article that talked about the location of Patterson's planned new home. The article mentioned the number of rooms and the modern conveniences intended for the home. It appeared money was no object for the project. The report, dated Mar 5, 1925, speculated about a completion date for the house before the end of the year.

The second article talked about the Ice Works and the outlook for the 1925/1926 season. Patterson, as a representative of the railroad, alluded to higher shipping costs. The Ice Works company said the higher prices put pressure on company profits. According to the reporter, the company planned to increase production to offset the higher costs.

Joel, reading between the lines, surmised Patterson personally profited on any increases. The third article was about a prominent Seven Lakes businessmen who, along with the Mayor, attended an official announcement ceremony for a national retail chain planning to open a store on Main Street. The store, according to the write-up, would help further bolster an already thriving business district in Seven Lakes. Patterson's name was listed as an attendee.

After reading the article, it reminded Joel about the column he had come across at the historical society called "Seven Lakes Residents." It was a gossip column highlighting the comings and goings of the town residents. The column gave him an idea, and he asked Cantey if she was familiar with it.

"Oh heavens, yes," she replied smiling, "I remember my mother reading it when I was younger, she would make comments about how so and so could afford to go gallivanting off to the cities at the drop of a hat."

"Do me a favor?" Joel said, "check the column for December of 1925 and see if it mentions the Patterson's being in town for the holidays."

"Alright, is there anything else you are looking for?" Canty asked, sensing he was on to something.

"No, just looking for any connection to Mary or Mr. Williams or both to Patterson in some way." Answered Joel.

Cantey returned to her desk, and the library fell into silence. Joel resumed his search through the letters and journals, hoping to find a thread to follow. Suddenly, Mrs. Cantey broke the silence.

"I found something." She nearly shouted. Joel thought it amusing that the person normally schussing others, was now the person breaking the unwritten rules of library etiquette. Making his way over to her desk, he found Cantey pointing to a small section of print on the microfiche screen. The image appeared to be a half-page of an old newspaper, and Joel could see woman's dresses and elixirs from an apothecary advertised on the page. Coming closer, he leaned in to view the article and started to read it aloud. "The Seven Lakes Grand

Hotel held their annual Christmas party last night, and the festivities went late into the evening. Notable people in attendance included Mayor Bradley, his wife Sally, and Mr. Patterson and his wife, Lucy.

Joel understood he was looking at the first possible connection of a person of interest to Mary. It was likely she would have attended the party, which ostensibly would have put her in the same room as Patterson. That fact was a far cry from a solution, but it was an exciting development. Also, Patterson's Shoreline Drive home was well within Joel's circle of probability as an acceptable distance for her to travel in the storm.

Joel had a better understanding of the hardships facing the residents from the letters he had read. There were several references in personal journals about the rugged men who worked the ice harvest and how the storm had stopped the operation until the tons of snow removed from the ice field. Labor costs for the company were already tight, and the increase in transportation costs ultimately would be borne by those who could least afford it, the workers. Patterson, who never got anywhere near the actual work, received his cut from the railroad, and by the looks of his new mansion, was doing pretty well for himself.

Joel gathered his stuff and thanked Mrs. Cantey for her help. She was pleased that he had entrusted her to help him in his search and assured him she was available to help in any way.

Joel walked across the parking lot, unlocked the door, and slid into the interior of the Bel Air. The car sitting in the frigid temperatures all morning felt like an icebox. The engine hesitated slightly before starting when turning the ignition key. Joel had already set the heat control levers to their maximum position and now waited for the first signs of warmth.

Sam sounded pleased when he called and readily agreed to meet him for breakfast in the morning. She said she would go in early and that he could pick her up at work.

"I believe there may have been significant progress today," Said Joel.

"So, I suppose you will make me wait until the morning?" Replied Sam.

"Exactly,"

CHAPTER 20

(December 22, 1925)

The threat of snow in Seven Lakes had been building throughout the day. Shortly after 4:00 pm, the first large flakes floated lightly to earth, taking their time before settling on fence posts, birdfeeders, dirt roads, or other random places exposed to the elements. Unlike a rainstorm that is accompanied by thunderclaps, flashes of lightning, and cold rushing downdrafts, snowstorms often start quietly, and with little fanfare.

At first, it looked like someone had painted everything with a brushstroke of white, and objects retained their form, but over the next 10 hours, only the most substantial items would still be recognizable.

Visibility between 4:00 and 6:00 pm was still reasonable despite the volume of snow falling because it fell in a mostly vertical direction in the calm air. A person standing near a street lamp on Main Street would surely have been impressed by the millions of illuminated flakes reflected in a halo around the light.

Shortly after 6:00 pm, winds picked up, lifting accumulated snow from unprotected surfaces and combining it with falling snow to create moving curtains of white, and reducing visibility to near zero. Familiar objects were starting to lose their edges and becoming a part of the new landscape sculpted by the storm.

There are beauty and silence within a snowstorm that is unlike anything else in nature. As the snow accumulates, the world becomes a quieter place, and actions ordinarily accompanied by sound, like a passing car, now appear surreal as it glides past with just a whisper.

Shoreline Drive, with its northern exposure, saw high-velocity winds coming across the unobstructed expanse of ice, which displaced large quantities of snow onto the embankment below the road.

Around 7:00 pm, Braden, the Seven Lakes Station Master, received notification that they held the 7:45 train in Fairview as a precaution. The engineer, not wanting to take a chance of stranding passengers in the 50 mile stretch of open plains between the two cities.

The drifts along Lakeshore Drive continued to gain in height. As they approached the elevation of the road, wind gusts blew off their tops, sending small avalanches of snow down Main Street to accumulate against any obstacle in its path.

Only one business in downtown remained open, a speakeasy located several blocks south of the lake, its hardcore regulars deciding it was a better place than home to ride out the storm.

Mary Benton, standing next to her fourth-floor window, leaned over her writing-table with both hands flat against its surface. She strained to see through the blackness beyond her window, trying to judge the severity of the storm. Her room had a lake view, but that was of no use tonight. The light from her table lamp illuminated a small area outside her window, and the only thing she could tell was the frantic pace in which snow hit against the glass. She could hear eerie moans from the roof as the wind rushed across exposed pipes and other openings, like instruments in a creepy symphony.

The outstretched fingers of her right hand rested lightly on the edge of a handwritten note she placed on the table. Presumably, the hotel staff had delivered it by slipping it beneath her door. Looking down at it now, she re-read it for the 3rd time. The cursive letters scrawled across the page were in bold flourishes, giving her the impression the writer completed it in haste.

"*Mary, we have not been formally introduced. I saw you at the Christmas party last night and would be grateful if you would agree to meet with me at my office tonight at 8:00 pm. The location is 4000 Shoreline Drive; it is the main offices of the Ice Works Company. – Charles Patterson.*"

Mary knew the proposed meeting was a bad idea and felt it fortunate the weather had deteriorated to a point where the meeting, however ill-advised, made even less sense in the prevailing conditions.

So why could she not tear it up? Why was it still on the table where she could read it? In retrospect, she knew her mother had made bad choices and had put herself and Mary in danger. So, why was she entertaining an invitation to meet a married man in a remote location alone at night?

CHAPTER 21

(December 22, 1925)

Mary, dressed in her warmest clothes, walked to the writing desk, picked up the note, and placed it back into its envelope, folding it in half, she put it into an inside pocket of her overcoat. She looked one more time out the window and the blackness beyond, before crossing the room and opening the door into the hallway. Stepping out, she pulled the door shut and locked it with her key.

As she made her way to the staircase, she pulled her hat down low to cover her ears and forehead. Her hair curling forward, pressed flat against her cheeks, and only a small amount of her face was still exposed. She moved quickly, forcing herself forward, trying to silence her inner voice of caution.

The hotel was unusually quiet, and when reaching the final set of stairs, and descending into the lobby, she saw only one employee behind check-in who was writing into a ledger style book. The woman looked up momentarily at Mary before resuming her work. Mary crossing the lobby, stood in front of the double doors to the outside. She felt a draft of cold air passing through unsealed crevices between the doors. Gusts of wind from the lake buffeted the hotel, seemingly testing its structural integrity. Mary could hear creaks and groans from the floors above, the wood frame hotel protesting the storm's onslaught.

Mary's indecision was palatable as she watched blowing snow move down the street in waves, now unsure if she should try to travel the required distance to the meeting.

Overcoming her apprehension, she pushed hard against the right side door and felt the wind causing it to resist. Pushing harder, she swung it out enough to allow her to step onto the porch, the door slamming shut with help from another blast of wind after letting go. Mary immediately felt cold all over and pulled her coat collar up as high as it would go to protect her neck while giving her hat another downward tug for good measure. Her clothes were not sufficient for the conditions, and in the back of her mind, she knew there was a possibility Patterson would not keep the appointment. Pushing the thought aside, she stepped off the porch and turned toward the lake.

The storm had already transformed the landscape, and there was no delineation between the hotel property, the road, or the previously exposed ice of Seven Lakes. There was already an accumulation of several inches and more in areas prone to drifting. The wind coming in large gusts, rushed through leafless branches, producing a sound similar to a roaring waterfall.

To reach her destination, Mary needed to travel Shoreline Drive until it terminated into the Ice Works property. She had seen a blurb in the newspaper days earlier about the ice harvesting season getting underway, but had not paid it much attention at the time.

Blowing snow off the ice had created large drifts along the shoreline, and Mary could see the tops drifting across the road. The road, hugging the shore, provided little in the way of protection from its northern exposure.

Mary couldn't remember a time of being this cold. The road after a time turned in a more northerly direction, with the wind now coming directly against her, the airborne ice crystals stinging her exposed skin, lips, and eyes. Anticipating the wind gusts, she turned her back into them to protect the exposed areas of her face, until it subsided.

The snow fell at a tremendous rate, and Mary could only make out basic shapes of objects in the distance. Crystals moving along the surface gave the impression that the whole road was in motion coming toward her. Trees, fences, and other structures had an out of focus look, and anything beyond a certain distance faded into white. She could see the shadow of a significant incline of uniform height in the woods running parallel to Shoreline Drive.

Mary, unsure of distance, started to worry about exposure. Lowering her chin shielded her face, but the angle, only allowed her to see a few feet of the road. Every few minutes, she looked up to make sure she had not strayed from the roadbed toward the lake or down the steep bank leading into the woods.

Mary judged the accumulation to now be near six inches, and after trudging through for ten more minutes, she looked up to see a two-story structure a hundred yards or so in the distance. There were larger indistinct structures beyond it that looked like looming dark shadows masked by the falling snow.

There was a light on in a second-story window of the building in the foreground, and Mary thought it a good sign that Patterson might still be there. The thought of being inside where it was warm became an all-consuming goal; her apprehension replaced by a will to survive.

Arriving at the front of the building, she stepped onto its wooden platform, and reached for the doorknob, but was unable to grip it with her numb fingers. Placing her other hand over the first, she was able to apply enough pressure to turn the knob, and the door swung inward. Entering into the dark space, she closed the door by leaning against it with her shoulder. Inside the dark entryway, she could barely make out a central hallway running toward the back of the building. The entry and hall were not well heated, but being protected from the wind and blowing snow was an immense improvement.

Feeling her way around the space, she found another door on the left side of the entry just past the front window. Rubbing her hands together vigorously, she brought a small amount of feeling back into her fingers, and this time was able to turn the knob. Inside the door, a dark staircase led to the second floor. Looking up the stairs, she could see a small amount of light leaking around a door on the right side of the landing.

Closing the door cast the stairwell into darkness, and Mary had to quietly feel her way up the stairs using the handrail as a guide.

Reaching the top and standing in front of the door, she could barely make out the words on the brass name-plate that said, "Patterson Enterprises" in bold letters. Mary could feel herself trembling; this time, it was a combination of nerves and the brutal cold she had endured.

CHAPTER 22

(December 22, 1925)

Timmy Williams was ten years old when snow began to fall in the early evening of December 22, 1925. He lived in a small two-story frame house a couple of blocks from the lake. For the most part, he did not live his life in the house; he lived habitually in his imagination. His bedroom was a place where the adventure took flight, and where book characters and made-up worlds came to life, protecting him from the harshness of the outside world.

Timmy's mom had died of what his dad called a "Bad Heart," when Timmy was seven, and since that time, the warmth she had once provided somehow seeped out of their home, leaving an emptiness in its place. His dad went through the motions of life by working during the day and frequenting speakeasies along Main Street during the evenings. He was not violent or mean-spirited, he had just lost his way, and no longer possessed the capacity to care for a son.

Timmy had learned to fend for himself, including making meals, and sometimes if his dad remembered to leave him money, he would go to a local diner near the lake where the wait-staff adopted him as one of their own. Seven Lakes was a small town, and people in small town's talk, so before long, his less than desirable home-life was public knowledge, and a few residents checked in on him from time-to-time.

His teacher, Ms. Stevenson, on his first week back in school after summer vacation, had asked him to stay after class during a Friday dismissal. When the rest of the kids had scattered in every direction after stampeding outside, she presented him with a brand new jacket. He did not realize adults like Ms. Stevenson were concerned for his welfare and thought the jacket to be a fortunate coincidence of timing since winter was just around the corner.

Timmy mostly kept to himself at school and tried to avoid calling attention to himself if possible. Experience taught him early, that attention for him, was usually not positive. He had a propensity for escaping into imaginary worlds and was mostly an outcast among his fellow students. He used this escape strategy anytime he found himself in an uncomfortable or painful situation. He loved to read books from the library and bought adventure magazines whenever he had enough money.

Tonight, standing next to his bedroom window, he watched the thick snowfall that looked to have already accumulated several inches in the yard and on the roof. He was excited about the prospect of finally being able to build snow forts in the yard, with this storm looking like the first real snow of the season. He had read a book over the summer about Shackleton's 1907 expedition to Antarctica on the Nimrod and could easily imagine himself as one of his brave explorers.

There was a small flat area just below his dormer window, and in warmer months, in the evenings, he would climb out and watch for activity on his block. The roof, steeply pitched, had about a 10-foot fall to the edge before dropping 12-feet to the ground. Sitting on the ledge during the summer months, he had often wondered what it might be like to slide down and launch himself from the edge. Of course, in his imagination, the flight time would be gloriously long, and his landing, flawless and without injury.

Tonight, as he watched the snow pile up, the prospect of actually sliding off the edge, and sailing blissfully through the air seemed somehow possible. Besides, he thought; conditions might not be this good for quite some time. Once on the ground, he would transform himself into a great arctic explorer. As he watched out the window, a large gust of wind picked up snow from the surface and moved it rapidly down the Street. For seconds, he could no longer see the houses on the other side of the Street. "That was great." He said under his breath; he loved the idea of invisibility where he could operate incognito from the rest of Seven Lakes.

Timmy lacing up his boots, pulled his jean pant legs down tightly around their tops; he had learned the hard way that without proper precautions, snow would find its way inside. He grabbed the jacket his teacher had given him off the back of his closet door; he liked that it had multiple pockets because explorers are required to carry many items for survival.

Picking up his knife from the desk, he slipped it into a top pocket and then pulling open the center drawer and finding his compass and flashlight, gave each a separate pocket for safekeeping. He thought about his slingshot for protection, but had not seen it since the summer, and could not take time to look for it now. Inside his closet, he found his gloves, a long scarf, and a stocking hat. After buttoning his jacket to the top, he wrapped the scarf around his neck two times and pulled it up, so it partially covered his face. Putting on his stocking hat, he pulled it down until it covered his ears, and as a last-minute check, patted his coat, making sure he had the items required for survival.

Walking to the window, he eased it open, and a flurry of flakes swirled in on a current of frigid air, the flakes settling on the wooden floor, quickly melted. Climbing out through the window opening onto the roof, he stood on the level space before closing the window behind him. Sitting down, he could feel the cold surface through his jeans. Dangling, his legs over the edge onto the pitched part of the roof, he used his hands to push up and scooted his bottom forward until he was sitting directly on the point where the pitched roof joined the flat surface. With one final look at his projected landing spot, he pushed up on his hands and pulled himself onto the slope with his legs. It was a slow start for the first couple of feet before rapidly gaining momentum and launching off the roof like an Olympic ski jumper, with his legs outstretched.

For Timmy, the couple of seconds spent sailing through the air gave him a sensation of flying he would never forget. Unlike the longer flight time and smooth landing of his imagination, the ground came up fast to meet him, and the speed of contact along with his forward momentum pitched him violently head-first against the snow and grass in a sprawling fashion. He had a moment of panic when he could n't catch his breath after hitting the ground, and when recovered, felt icy snow against his neck and chest where it had breached the jacket's collar when sliding on his stomach for a half a dozen feet. Picking himself up, he unbuttoned the coat and removed the snow from inside, before brushing off his pants to keep them dry.

He was pleased there weren't any signs that the storm was letting up, and if anything, it felt like the volume of falling snow may have even increased. He started in the direction of the lake where he could explore the shoreline and plan his route across the northern plain in search of the South Pole.

As he approached Shoreline Drive, the storm revealed more of its ferocity as it moved large swaths of snow from the ice, across Shoreline drive, depositing it against immovable objects like walls fences and trees. The wind gusts came at quicker intervals near the lake, and with significantly increased velocity, and out on the ice, conditions resembled a constant white-out condition.

His Street dead-ended into Shoreline Drive, where the land on either side was undeveloped and heavily wooded. There was an old rock wall running perpendicular to Shoreline Drive, an indication that the property had once been an old farmstead or estate. Snow drifts on the lake-facing side of the wall were nearly even with its top, but the backside, practically clear of snow, provided protection and shelter from the brutally cold wind.

Timmy hunkering down behind the wall, from time-to-time peered over its top where small airborne crystals driven on the wind stung his face and eyes. The third time he raised himself to peer over the edge of the wall, he saw something unexpected. A woman alone, dressed in a long dark coat, and a black hat was walking in the middle of the road-bed. The woman leaned slightly forward as if she was pushing against a steady headwind. She held her head low, scrunched down inside her coat collar, and appeared to be looking almost straight at the ground.

Timmy thought this new development might prove more impressive than his arctic expedition, besides conditions on the ice looked way too dangerous. She might be a spy, he thought, or a smuggler using the storm as cover.

He decided to follow her at a distance, hoping she would reveal her secret rendezvous location. Peering over the wall again, he could see he would need to move from his shelter soon. The woman making steady progress along the road had already become harder to see through the falling snow.

As he moved from behind the protective wall, he felt it would be safest to stay on the left side of the road near the woods. He could use a technique he had learned in an adventure magazine, whereby a person tailing a suspect moves from object to object, staying out of the suspect's line of sight, in case the person was to turn and look back.

The Ice Works could be the only logical destination for anyone traveling this far along Shoreline Drive; there just wasn't anything else out there. It made sense in Timmy's mind; It was undoubtedly a remote out of way place.

Timmy played in these woods 100's of times and was familiar with most of the area along the Drive. He knew the spur line cut away from the main, near the edge of Seven Lakes, and angled through the woods toward the lake and the Ice Works operation. The railroad parked rail cars inside the Ice Works property during harvest season, where they awaited loads of ice for shipment to the west.

The spur, Timmy thought, would be a great place to stay hidden, while still having a commanding view of the Ice Works facility since it traversed the high point of the ridge above the operation.

Timmy watched the woman, barely visible now, reach a point in the road where it curved in a more northerly direction. Staying hidden, inside the tree line, he quickened his pace, moving forward in short increments. When he reached the curve, he took one last look at the woman in the distance, before detouring into the woods toward the elevated spur line.

Timmy sliding down a small embankment into the woods, cut a path through the snow as he ran toward the elevated spur. He slipped several times, attempting to climb the steep grade before finally reaching the top. The plateau, not much more extensive than the width of the tracks, fell off sharply on either side.

The snow had filled in between the ties until just the tops of the rails were still visible. The tracks in the distance, curved gently to the right, as they moved closer to Shoreline Drive and the entrance to the Ice Works. Timmy carefully walked on the ties between the rails, trying to judge their spacing as he went.

Halfway into the curve, he regained sight of the woman, just as she crossed through the perimeter fence onto the Ice Works property. Timmy traveling another 100 feet or so down the line saw the light in a second-story window of the companies office building. The building, located approximately 50 yards inside the perimeter fence, was probably her destination since he lost track of her shortly after she crossed onto the property.

Timmy, continuing down the tracks, saw two boxcars looming in the distance. The wind, still brutal off the lake, caused him to search for shelter to limit his exposure.

As he approached the boxcars, he saw a small shack-like structure that looked as if it had been cobbled together with wood scraps and stood just to the side of the tracks. The shack, open on one side, was closed-in on the lake-facing side and had a small dirty window hung at a slight angle. The three-walled structure offered him protection while still affording him a view of the yard below.

He pressed his face close to the window and stared down at the office building in hopes of catching a glimpse of the probable illicit dealings taking place. Beyond the office building, further down the hill, he saw smoke rising from a warming barrel. The barrel, loaded with wood and lit on fire during shifts, provided the ice workers a place to warm their hands.

The woman in Timmy's estimation had been inside the building for at least 15 minutes when he noticed a set of lights approaching from Shoreline Drive. He watched the lights come closer, the headlamps illuminating the falling snow in their path. It was an automobile moving along Shoreline Drive. The car stopped just short of the entrance to the Ice Works, before extinguishing its lights.

"Something is going on down there," Timmy said under his breath. In his imagination, these people were secret operatives conducting clandestine work inside the building and cleverly using the storm to shield their operation from prying eyes. It was up to him to find out who they were and in what type of illegal activity they were involved.

It had been another ten minutes since the second person arrived when he again

Detected movement near the office building. This time it was on the opposite side of the building, where two figures close together, walked with urgency toward the large storage warehouse standing a hundred or so feet to the east: the structure used to store ice for the local population of Seven Lakes. The two figures, close together, almost appeared as one, as they moved through the storm.

There was a delay when they reached the entrance and appeared to be having trouble opening the oversized door. The door, finally swinging open, revealed a black interior, and one of two moved inside the darkness. The second figure, hesitating, stooped down to pick up something leaning against the wall before stepping through the doorway and pulling the large door shut.

Timmy could feel a sharp pain in his fingertips from the cold. Despite the mysterious activity below, the desire for warmth was beginning to override the excitement of his adventure. Staring out the dirty window, he thought it might be time to start making his way back home to the warmth of his bedroom. He was about to leave the shelter, and retrace his steps along the tracks when the warehouse door swung back open and a single figure, holding something close, stepped back into the storm.

The figure moved down the hill toward the lakeshore, and stopping at the smoldering warming barrel dropped whatever they were holding inside. The person then returned to the warehouse, went inside, and closed the door.

Timmy, curious about the bundle, felt like if he could get to the barrel without being seen, it would allow him a chance to see what the person had dropped inside. It would also give him a chance to warm his frozen hands if there was any heat left inside.

There wasn't much cover between the buildings and barrel, and cutting across the yard, he risked exposure to both the office building and the warehouse. A narrow strip of woods running along the outside perimeter fence looked to be the best route for staying hidden.

Ten minutes later, Timmy jumped down from the fence onto the Ice Works side of the property and remained in a crouched position while looking back up the hill to see if anyone was looking in his direction. Seeing nobody, he stayed low, making his way across the open space and sliding the last several feet until in position behind the barrel. He was thankful that the outside metal still had warmth and pressed his gloves against its sides, waiting for the heat to reach his fingers.

After a few minutes crouched behind the barrel, Timmy raised himself just enough to peer inside the container. It was dark, the embers providing just enough illumination to see an object against the side nearest him. Reaching inside, he grabbed what felt like cloth, and pulled the object out and dropping it in the snow when he saw that the bottom was red from being on top of the embers. There was a hissing noise, and steam rose from the snow where it landed.

He was disappointed to discover it was just clothes, he had hoped for something more exciting like secret documents. Making a closer examination of the clothes, he saw that it was held together with black lace material, tightly wrapped and tied off in a knot. Pulling off one of his gloves, he retrieved his pocket knife and tried to cut the bundle loose. He had only been able to tear through one layer of the knot with his dull blade when he heard a door slam from ontop the hill. Grabbing the partially cut piece with his hand, he tore it away from the garment. Carefully peering around the side of the barrel, he saw a bigger person moving from the office toward the warehouse. Stowing his knife and the torn piece of lace in his jacket, he pushed the bundle up and over the side of the barrel, where it sent a small cloud of ash into the air. Keeping the barrel between him and whoever the people were, Timmy moved backward toward the lake, staying as low to the ground as possible.

Approaching the shoreline, he noticed that an open channel cut in the ice stretched out into the lake. Workers use open water to float ice blocks toward the conveyor. The water, black against the night sky, looked inhospitable as the storm whipped its surface into a frenzy. A shiver ran through Timmy before turning from the lake and heading for home.

CHAPTER 23

(December 22, 1925)

Mary lightly knocked on the outer frame of Patterson's door. At first, there was silence, and then what sounded like a chair scraping against a wooden floor, followed by footsteps coming toward the door. When the door opened, the same impeccably dressed man she recognized from the party greeted her through bloodshot eyes.

"Mary," he said, "Come in, come in. I was not sure if you would make it here in such dreadful weather."

Mary felt sure he had made inquiries about her because of the way he used her name as if they were previous acquaintances, even though never formally introduced.

"Come in," he repeated, stepping aside to allow her into the small entry.

"Please, take off your coat and sit near the fire to warm up." The office was inviting and warm, and Mary looking around at the space moved past Patterson into the main room. The room, richly decorated with artwork and beautiful furnishings, felt more like a home than an office. In front of the fireplace, two leather chairs angled toward the fire sat on top of an oriental rug. Floor to ceiling built-in shelves took up a large portion of the far wall and filled with all manner of items, including awards, presumably from Patterson's accomplishments.

Mary sat down on the edge of one of the leather chairs with its back to the entry, still wearing her coat. She turned in, so she mostly faced the flames. The lively fire above a large bed of embers indicated it had been burning for quite some time. The warmth was so welcoming; she relaxed for the first time that evening.

She could hear the sound of clinking glassware from somewhere across the room, and glancing in the direction, saw Patterson in front of a small cabinet splashing brown liquid into two glasses from a clear decanter. Mary turned back to the fire as Patterson closed the cupboard and walked over to where she was seated. Reaching the side of her chair, Patterson handed one of the partially filled glasses. "This will help warm your insides," he said. Mary's hand trembled as she reached for the glass and with Patterson so close; she again felt nervous and apprehensive about the purpose of the meeting.

Taking a sip of the pungent-smelling drink, Mary is taken aback by its awful flavor and surprised at the warm sensation it produced traveling down her throat.

Patterson, smiling at her evident inexperience with liquor, sat down in the chair opposite hers.

"Mary, I am so pleased you came, I thought the severity of the storm might prove too much of an obstacle." Mary, turning in her chair, to face him, asked, "How do you know me?" Patterson, still smiling, said rather ominously, "It's my business to know about people. I have found in life, the more you know about a person, and their motivations, the better chance you have for a positive relationship." Mary nodded before taking another sip of her drink; she felt her body beginning to relax.

Looking across at Patterson, she asked: "What do you think motivates me?"

Patterson liked her directness, and being uncharacteristically truthful, replied, "I will have to admit; you are a bit of a mystery, nobody in Seven Lakes or Fairview seems to know anything about you." The fact that he had checked up on her in Fairview was a surprise, and somewhat worrying.

"I am not from Fairview," Mary said, Confirming what Patterson already suspected. "What is your interest in me?"

Patterson, unprepared for her question, and overwhelmed by her natural beauty, decided to lay some cards on the table.

"When I saw you at the party, I could not look away. There was an inner drama playing out within you against the backdrop of the celebration that I found fascinating. You were physically in the room, but somewhere else entirely in your mind. I am a student of people, especially beautiful women, and I was naturally curious about your story."

"May I take your coat?" Patterson offered for the second time. Mary, who had forgotten she was still wearing it, stood up, unbuttoned it, and handed it to him. Patterson, in a somewhat unsteadily fashion, caused by the day's heavy drinking, retreated to the entry hall where he hung her coat near the door.

When he returned, he started asking Mary the same questions she always struggled to answer. Where was her home? What brought her to Seven Lakes? Did she have family in the area? Mary responded with half-truths, made up relations, and the fabricated stories she used successfully in the past. She portrayed a life of being on the road with her mother, who she said was an entertainer. Mary explained how they traveled between towns, only staying one or two nights, before moving on. When her mother died of pneumonia, Mary was 13 and went to live with her mom's sister near the Canadian border.

Mary could hear the wind outside; the snow hitting the windows made a slight ticking noise against the glass. Patterson's interest in her, so far, seemed genuine, but she still did not know to what end. Whatever his intentions, she would try to be as open as she could manage, she was out of options, and a person of Patterson's wealth could provide her with an advantage.

With the wind howling outside and the snow continuing to pile up, the office felt like a secret hideaway — sumptuous furnishings, low lighting, and a magical potion that both warmed her insides while numbing her reality. There was a feeling of seclusion and safety from the outside world here.

Patterson's desire growing more intense as time passed, devoured her body with his eyes each time she turned toward the fire.

"So, Mary, why did you come here tonight?" Patterson asked. Mary, surprised by his question, said, "You invited me."

"I know," Patterson said, "what I am asking is why you came? You are a businesswoman, are you not?" Mary, silent, looked into the fire. "You are here because you want something from me, isn't that true?" Mary could only manage to shake her head side to side; while avoiding his stare. He saw her silence as a sign of weakness and felt he had made the correct assessment, and now was time to close the deal.

Patterson leaned back and reached inside his vest pocket, produced a $20.00 gold piece. Placing the gleaming coin on the small table between them, he slid it toward Mary. "I am a businessman also," he said, staring at the buttons on the front of her blouse. "I know who you are Mary; I see your type every day in all of the crappy little towns along the rail lines, you are a prostitute who is looking for a rich mark like me to pay handsomely for your favors."

It was not a question, and his words hit her like a punch to the stomach, "a prostitute" her worst fears were being realized, she was in too deep. She shook her head sideways again, unable to form any words in response.

“Don’t play innocent, Patterson said in a low guttural voice, his arousal and proximity to her getting the better of him. “You have been staying at that hotel looking for someone exactly like me to take care of you. Unfortunately for you, I am wise to the ways of the world and how your type operates, so why don’t you show me what I am willing to pay for.” He said as he dropped his gaze back to the front of her blouse, “why don’t you unbutton your pretty white blouse and show me what a little whore you are.”

Mary blinked back tears at the harshness of his words, her vision blurred, caused a flickering effect as firelight reflected off the surface of the coin. Patterson’s face was out of focus, and the disorienting effect of the liquor had rendered the room askew. “Stand up and unbutton your blouse,” he repeated in a more menacing tone.

Mary willed herself out of her chair, maintaining some distance, as her trembling hands unbuttoned her blouse. Looking past Patterson, she tried to forget he was in the room. When she had undone the last button, the garment parted a few inches revealing a black lace camisole.

Mary could feel his eyes on her but could not bear to look at his face; instead, she focused on an oil painting of a rocky shoreline hanging behind his desk. The picture lit from below with a covered lamp, made its vibrant colors stand out in the dim room. It was a peaceful scene with a shoreline in the foreground, and calm blue-green waters, and a clear blue sky.

Patterson was saying something in the background that she couldn’t hear, and now with a raspy voice, he repeated. “Come closer.” He said. Mary, standing motionless, tried to concentrate.

“Come closer,” Patterson said again in a less demanding voice.

Mary took a step toward him without taking her eyes from the painting. She understood she was entering a point of no return, and her inexperience and his change of personality frightened her.

When she was within his reach, Patterson, in one swift motion, reached up, and grabbing the front of her lace camisole, jerked it down with such force that both of the thin shoulder straps ripped from the fabric leaving Mary exposed to the waist.

Despite the swiftness of his assault, things for Mary were moving in slow motion, with sounds garbled, she felt detached from the room, but could somehow still see everything that was happening.

Looking down, she saw Patterson molesting her breasts, her ripped camisole hanging from her waist, and her blouse pushed halfway down her arms had the effect of pinning her arms to her sides. She felt pain from his groping, but that too was distant and detached.

Looking back at the painting, she tried to recapture its calm but could not concentrate as a new pressure against her thighs forced her legs apart. Alarms were going off inside her head, telling her she was in real danger from the brutality of his assault. Looking to the left, she did not readily recognize the panicked reflection she saw in an oval mirror above the fireplace. The image shattered her protective illusion of detachment.

Mary, looking back at the painting, saw the calming scene had turned violent, as she envisioned her own naked, twisted body washed up between the rocks like common trash. The image of her mother, hidden in the recesses of her memory, flooded in, the injustice and brutality that took her mother when Mary was 13. Tears welled up in her eyes, remembering the horror she witnessed. Gaining strength, she muttered, "nobody deserves to die in that way," to herself

She could hear Patterson's heavy breathing as he struggled to remove her remaining clothes. Realizing the danger in her predicament, she jerked furiously backward, catching Patterson off-guard and temporarily freeing herself from his grasp. Patterson lunging for her was limited in movent by the arm of the chair. Mary remaining just out of reach continued to back away, creating an ever-larger separation and looking behind her for the door.

Patterson, sensing her flight, stood up too quickly, his face flushed with anger, the sudden motion causing him to become lightheaded, gave Mary enough time to reach the entrance hallway.

Patterson, regaining his balance started across the room, and Mary, unable to retrieve her jacket, grabbed the doorknob and twisting it hard, swung it open, and passed through into the cold dark storage space before slamming the door behind her.

Cold invaded her exposed body, and she grasped the edges of her blouse, having no time to fasten it properly, she tried to hold it together. Mary couldn't see a thing in the hallway once the door shut, and holding her blouse with her left hand, she frantically searched the wall for the handrail with her right. There was a crash from inside the office, like something hitting the floor, followed by a low groan. Mary's panicked search ended as her hand finally grasped the smooth surface of the wooden rail. Mary had no idea how she would escape into the cold with barely any clothes; she just knew she had to put distance between herself and Patterson. Pressing herself close to the railing, she hurried down the steps, the material of her blouse making an shhh sound against the rail as she went.

It felt like she was descending into an abyss and, at any second, expected the office door to fling open, and Patterson to follow. She advanced down the stairs in blackness, sliding her hand forward on the railing before taking each step. Believing she was near the landing, she pressed her hand forward, but this time it slipped over the top of another cold hand that was also holding onto the railing. Mary, letting out an audible shriek, recoiled backward, and losing her balance, fell hard against the stairs, a sharp pain surging through her lower back.

Looking up, she could barely see an outline of a figure above her. The black shadow leaned in toward her, and Mary pressed herself against the steps, the pain shooting up her spine. Mary turned her head to the side, trying to avoid the dreadful encounter. She heard a low whisper, and despite her fear, strained to listen.

"Mary," the voice repeated, "you're in danger here, I can help you." Mary heard more noise from the office above. "We have to leave now," the voice whispered with more urgency. Reaching down toward Mary, the figure placed a hand on her arm and assisted her up, the sharp pain in her back protesting as she stood.

Despite her fear, she forced herself to focus on the task of separating herself from Patterson. She had seen something in his eyes when he caused her physical pain and realized the danger of being an object of his sick pleasure.

"I know where we will be safe," the person said in a low voice. Mary could tell now that the unseen person was a woman. She had been standing at the bottom of the stairs, almost as if waiting for Mary to come down. Mary, holding the woman's forearm, grimaced as she took the final step onto the landing. The woman led her through the doorway into the entry area, and then through the main door outside. The cold attacked Mary's scantily clad body, and she immediately began shivering from the exposure. She could only see the side of the woman's face because of her scarf. Mary, looking ahead, saw they were heading toward the taller wooden structure she had seen beyond the office building when she arrived. Reaching the structure, the woman left Mary's side to open the large door. Once opened, she motioned Mary inside. There was no light in the interior, and as Mary went through the doorway, she nearly missed seeing that the floor dropped several feet, barely avoiding a fall that would have sent her sprawling onto the dirt.

The woman picking up an object leaning against the side of the structure followed Mary inside before pulling the large door shut behind her.

CHAPTER 24

(Present)

Joel opened his eyes to a pitch-black room, lying still, he sensed something external had disrupted his sleep, but everything around him was quiet.

The woman had returned in his dream, and she had been so close, he could look into her eyes. She had a beautiful face, but her expression was one of sadness. He could smell her perfume, and the scent seemed somehow familiar.

A sudden chill ran through his body as he realized the scent, like a fine mist, still hovered in the air now. Staring into the blackness, he wondered if someone was in his room, standing motionless, just out of reach.

Quietly, he lifted his arm from beneath the sheet and lightly ran his fingers along the headboard, searching for the push button switch to turn on the reading lamp. Finding it, he pressed it in hard, flooding the immediate area with light. He could not tell if it was his expectation or because of the sudden transition, that for an instant, he saw shadowy movement in his peripheral vision.

Slipping out of bed, he thoroughly searched the room, and finding nothing, returned to sit on the bed's edge. He tried to recall the sequence of events that had brought him face-to-face with the woman. This dream was different, more personal. In the past, the woman was mostly obscure and distant, but tonight, she was close, and her haunting presence was both beautiful and frightening.

Picking up his phone from the bedside table, he hoped to see a call or text from Sam. There were no new calls or messages. He carried the phone into the bathroom and set it on the granite vanity before turning the shower control to its hottest setting. When steam began rising within the glass enclosure, he stepped inside and let the heated water and steam engulf him for the next ten minutes.

Cutting off the water, he slid open the glass door and saw a ghostly reflection of himself in the fogged mirror opposite the shower. Stepping onto the marble tile, he froze in place. The smell of perfume in the bathroom was cloyingly strong; the scent mixing with steam filled the room. Joel had an uneasy feeling as he tried to rationalize the source of the smell.

Grabbing a towel, he wrapped it around his waist before reaching for the doorknob. Jerking his hand back after gripping the knob, he was momentarily shocked by its freezing temperature. Grabbing it again, he twisted it fast and pushed the door open into the main room.

He shivered violently from the cold as he surveyed the room. Scattered across the floor were every pillow, linen, and anything else that had previously been on a horizontal surface. The room was freezing from subzero air pouring through the wide-open balcony doors. After his initial shock, he rushed across the room to close and secure the balcony doors. Stepping around the items on the floor, he returned to the bathroom, where the cold had not entirely permeated the space. Picking up his phone from the counter, he tapped Sam's number. She answered on the first ring, sounding happy to hear from him until she heard his voice.

"Joel, what's wrong?" She asked.

"Something is going on; I am not sure I can explain," his voice trailing off as if he was working on the problem as they talked.

"Joel, what is it, your scaring me?" Goosebumps are raising on her arms.

"No, no, I am not in danger," he said, trying to reassure her.

"It's my room; it doesn't make sense."

"What doesn't make sense, what about your room?" Sam asked warily.

"I had another dream, the same woman, in the middle of it, something woke me up. The room was dark, I couldn't see anything, but I had a sense somebody was there, standing in the darkness." Sam's fear escalated, but she tried to remain calm. "When I switched on the light, I thought I saw something move near the entry, but when I searched the room, nothing was out-of-place."

"Could it have been your imagination, since you were just waking up?" Sam asked, looking for a logical explanation.

"That's what I thought too," Joel said in a way that implied there was more to the story.

"Sam." Joel said in a severe tone, "in the dream; she was right in front of me, I saw her, she seemed so real, I could smell her perfume." Joel paused, "When I woke up, the scent of her perfume was in my room." Sam covered her mouth with her hand, stopping a small panicked sound, trying to escape from her throat.

"Where are you?" she asked anxiously.

"I am still here, in the room, in the bathroom. There is something else." Sam was sure she did not want to hear something else.

"I took a shower, and when I finished and opened the door into the main room, the balcony doors were wide open, and everything, including all the bedding, was on the floor."

"Joel," Sam interrupted, "You have to leave, somebody is messing with you; you could be in danger."

"I don't think whoever did this intended to harm me if they did, they missed an opportunity when I was sleeping," Ignoring what Joel was saying, Sam, asked, "Can you leave, can you come to Fairview? I planned to go to the museum early; you could come here."

"I have a couple of things I want to look at this morning, but can leave after that,"

"Honestly Joel, I am worried, promise me you will be careful. What about the police?"

Joel paused, "I don't know, I am not sure I am up for all that would entail."

"Men!" Sam said indignantly, "You're all alike. Call me when you leave Seven Lakes,"

"I'll be careful," Joel said, before saying goodbye.

Getting dressed, Joel didn't bother picking up the items on the floor except for his wallet. Standing for a moment in front of the balcony doors, he watched low gray clouds moving in from the north — the predictions were for severe winter weather by the early evening.

Calling down to the front desk, he requested the valet retrieve his car, and a short time later, with the interior still warming up, turned right from the hotel to the light at Main and Shoreline Drive and then left onto Shoreline Drive. Traffic was sparse, and the large estates fronting on the lake looked like silent sentinels awaiting the approaching storm.

After driving along the shore for approximately a mile, Shoreline Drive turned sharply left, away from the lake. Joel knew from old maps that this area comprised the original Ice Works property. About a half-block further up, a dead-end cross street had a rusted chain-link fence running its length in front of old buildings in varying states of disrepair. The side fence for the property continued south on Shoreline Drive for another block, and ending with a sign marking the "Old Spur Line Walking Trail." Just past the trail, Joel pulled into a dirt lot designated for trail use and parked his car.

Getting out, he walked back to the trail and followed it along the back fence of the property. Not realizing he had gained elevation coming up Shoreline Drive, he was surprised to see a commanding view of the former Ice Works property and the lake beyond. The large wooden windowless structure inside the fence to his left looked to be the original ice house the reporter, Sorenson, told him about and a narrower two-story structure straight ahead, the companies old administration building.

Joel looking closely at the fence as he walked, searched for a breach he could exploit to get inside. After 50 feet or so, he saw a section of chain link had been cut halfway up from the ground. The breach, about ten feet from the trail, was several feet lower in elevation. Joel looking to see if anyone else was about, detoured down to the fence.

Crouching near the breach, he didn't notice his cell phone hanging precariously from his pocket. Getting on all fours, he crawled through the opening, his phone tumbling silently into the dead grass along the fence line.

Standing up inside the fence, he started toward the administration building, unaware he no longer had his phone.

Sorenson was right about the vandalization, all of the windows throughout the administration building had broken panes, and looking through one of the openings, he saw colorful graffiti-covering practically every inch of the interior.

According to information, Marty found when searching railroad records, Patterson kept an office in this very building during the time Mary was in Seven Lakes.

The ice house, a tall wooden structure with no windows, reminded Joel of the towering grain elevators built near the rail lines of small Minnesota towns. The narrow door like openings running up the center of the structure used for loading in the ice looked to be missing the original closures and now were haphazardly boarded up. A more significant door in the lower-left corner had a thick piece of wood running through black iron brackets holding it shut.

Pushing against the board, he was able to slide it until one end cleared the door frame bracket, allowing the door to swing outward — the air inside smelled of damp earth.

Joel stepping into the dark space saw a railing with several steps leading down to a dirt floor about four feet below ground level. Cobblestones formed the foundation walls, and the building was mostly empty, from what he could see from the light coming through the open door. Joel wished he had grabbed the LED flash-light from his car, and instinctively feeling his pocket, noticed his phone missing. Checking the rest of his pockets, he tried to recall if he had left it in the car.

Joel walking cautiously across the dirt floor was near the mid-dle when he noticed the narrow channel of light from the doorway collapsing into darkness, followed by the solid sound of wood collid-ing. At first, he thought the wind had caught the door, but now hear-ing the sound of a board sliding into place, he made a mad, blind dash toward the door, only to find it secured fast when he arrived.

Joel, without his phone, was angry at himself for not taking precautions after what had happened in his room. Somebody was not happy about him being in Seven Lakes, and whoever it was, must have followed him here.

As his eyes started to become accustomed to the dark interior, he surveyed the structure, looking for possible weak areas that could offer an escape.

CHAPTER 25

(Present)

TJ Shaffer was not feeling well when he came home from school at 3:00 pm. Seeking the comfort of his room. His new Popular Science magazine had arrived earlier in the week and was sitting on his night-stand with an intriguing picture of a deep-water sub exploring the depths of the Pacific. Grabbing the magazine, he kicked off his shoes and climbed fully clothed under his comforter. It was one of those days where he was unable to get warm, and after a few minutes under the cover, he realized the magazine would have to wait as sleep overtook him.

Outside TJ's window, a brief snow flurry filled the air with large flakes and then disappeared as quickly as it had started. The weather in Seven Lakes had been deteriorating all day and, the predictions were for a significant winter storm to sweep into the area, beginning in the early evening, and bringing with it, the first major snowfall of the season.

CHAPTER 26

(Present)

Carefully searching the interior walls of the Ice House, it became abundantly clear, the building had been well built — construction in those days used heavy lumber and a lot of it. The building would also have required extra walls for insulation, and that accommodation added a whole other level of sturdiness.

Joel suspected the door like openings used to load in the ice blocks, might provide his best chance of escape. He had noticed a couple of the openings had sloppily tacked up boards across them that looked far less sturdy than the main structure. Looking up, he could see daylight between some of the boards higher up on the wall.

Running his hand along the top of the cobblestone wall, he felt a small ledge, less than three inches in width from the interior edge to the beginning of the wood sill. It would be challenging to stand on such a thin ledge without a hand-hold, but the light was not good enough to visually locate one. He would have to work by feel to get himself into a position where he would have a chance to escape.

CHAPTER 27

(Present)

There was no one in Mr. Williams's room at the nursing home when he opened his eyes at 4:00 pm. Williams had struggled with nightmares his whole life, and after his dementia diagnoses, his day-to-day cognitive health had gone down fast. Now, in addition to his dreams, paranoia and an alternate reality filled his waking hours, and it was a world off-limits to outsiders.

The figure he saw standing beside his bed looking down at him was straight out of one of his nightmares. He opened his mouth to scream, but no sound escaped, his eyes went wide in search of someone to intervene, the smell of dampness and decay hung heavy in the air. The figure leaned in close; its face inches from his forcing him to look into the blackness of its hollow eyes as the stench of rot filled his nostrils and throat. Williams, shut his eyes, desperate for it to be over, and suddenly it was. After more than 100 years of faithfully beating, his heart stopped.

CHAPTER 28

(Present)

TJ tossed and turned in a fitful sleep as he dreamed about playing boot-hockey on the ice of Seven Lakes. The player's hockey sticks steering the puck-moving it up and down the ice, with neither team able to get it near their opponent's net.

TJ intercepted a pass and breaking through their defenses, had a clear path to the goal. An unseen player blindsided him with a hard check from the left, that sent both him and the puck sliding out-of-bounds—the boundaries designated by hats, scarfs, and anything else the boys could use as markers.

The puck traveled another ten yards out of bounds, and as TJ stepped and slid to retrieve it, he hit a rough patch that caused him to lose his balance and pitch forward face-first onto the ice. He slid several feet on his stomach and could hear laughter from the other boys.

TJ's face inches from the ice when he came to a stop, found himself looking in horror into the eyes of a woman frozen just below the surface. TJ started to yell but stopped himself, as ridicule flooded his memory. Pushing violently against the ice with his gloved hands, he tried to escape her frozen stare. His legs entangled limited his movement. Jerking his body to the right, he felt the ice give way beneath him, and for a second, experienced weightlessness before crashing hard onto his bedroom floor. The jolt woke TJ from the dream. Lying there on the floor, tangled in his comforter, a thin film of sweat covered his face and chest. Something in the back of his mind told him he needed to take care of an unresolved problem.

CHAPTER 29

(Present)

There was no question in Sam's mind that the snow was coming faster and with more intensity than when she had left Fairview at 5:00 pm. Visibility seemed to degrade by the minute, and all of her senses were on high alert. Reducing her speed, she stared hard between the wipers, praying she would not plow into the backend of a stalled car. She held her body rigid, her knuckles white from gripping the steering wheel.

Outside, the landscape disappeared under a blanket of white, and depth perception diminished with the sameness of it all. Sam felt vulnerable inside the car, its glass, metal, and plastic construction no longer felt substantial enough to protect her from the storm and the vastness of the rural landscape.

She couldn't see the farmhouses she knew dotted the landscape, her world shrinking as the storm closed in around her. Signs and objects near the highway appeared like quick fade-in shots on film. It was hard to judge progress without familiar landmarks, and the ones she could see had become distorted.

She was only half-listening to a voice on NPR reporting a national story that felt worlds away from her reality. She told herself to relax, everything would be ok, but she was not convinced. She couldn't shake the feeling that something had gone wrong in Seven Lakes. She had not been able to reach Joel all day, and that, coupled with the incident at the hotel, made it impossible to suppress her fear.

A soft glow in the distance and her odometer told her she was approaching the town of Stanley. Stanley, the approximate halfway point between Fairview and Seven Lakes, appeared out of the gloom in a sequence of lighted areas looking disjointed and out of place. She eased off the accelerator as she drove through a residential section, and glancing at her dashboard, double-checked the gas level, not wanting to become stranded through negligence.

There was little activity in Stanley, a gas station, and a restaurant the only businesses open. It had only been five minutes from the leading edge of town before its outer edge faded to black in her rear-view mirror, and she once again found herself closed in by a storm that had taken possession of the rural landscape.

She heard the start of a weather report on the radio, and turned up the volume from her steering wheel, not wanting to take her eyes off the narrowing strip of asphalt. Her wipers made a rumbling noise when moving up and to the left as they removed snow from the dry glass.

The predictions for this storm had changed several times during the day, but now forecasters were calling for a significant snow event with the potential of 12 to 18 inches.

Sam tried to gauge what had already fallen, but it was impossible to get a read with the flatlands moving past at 45 mph.

CHAPTER 30

(Present)

TJ stared at his bedroom ceiling, trying to forget the nightmare that had thrown him onto his bedroom floor. He thought about the night on the ice with his brother and his friends. The eerie face had appeared from deep within the ice. Had it been an illusion? Everything happened fast.

TJ's older brother, Derrick, played basketball on the school team, and tonight the squad had traveled to a small town about an hour from Seven Lakes, and he wouldn't be home until late. TJ liked having an older brother who could protect him, even though sometimes he needed protection from his brother.

The idea of going back out on the ice was something that had been on his mind since the night of the incident; the newspaper article had brought a lot teasing and ridicule from his classmates, and he wished he could prove them wrong.

Venturing out on the ice at night alone was entirely out of character for TJ, he usually avoided uncomfortable situations at any cost. His home was not far from the lake, and looking out his bedroom window, he could see snow flying rapidly past the corner street-lamp.

CHAPTER 31

(Present)

Joel was thankful for his gloves, he had already suffered a bruised knee and scraped shins from multiple unsuccessful attempts to scale the cobblestone wall, and stand on its narrow ledge. Without his gloves, his hands would have been cut and scraped as well from grabbing its surface as he fell back onto the dirt floor.

He had come close on his last attempt, his hand partially closing around something substantial that felt promising for scaling the wall. He searched the wall near the door where the small platform, was even with the top of the foundation. Still, if he could find a way to move up the wall, it was too far to the side of the openings to do any good.

Crouching at the base of the wall, his knee throbbing, he rested before his next attempt. He had a good idea of where the handhold was and would need to maintain his balance on the ledge long enough to find it again.

CHAPTER 32

(Present)

Sam finally reached Seven Lakes, relieved that she had made it without incident. Her first order of business, to locate Joel; he was still not answering his phone. She turned left onto Main Street through an empty intersection controlled by a flashing yellow caution. The backend of her car started to slide sideways, and she quickly spun the steering wheel in the direction of the slide as a countermeasure to straighten back up.

A plow had cleared a single car width down the middle of Main Street, and she stayed within the path, driving slowly on the deserted street. Where in the hell is Joel? Sam said, half aloud. If Sam hadn't believed him to be a street-wise detective, she would have been more panicked. It was hard to imagine him getting into a bad situation in Seven Lakes, but the fact remained that she had not heard from him since the incident that morning in his hotel room.

The snow coming at her windshield was nearly horizontal in its trajectory as she drove toward the lake. She knew conditions on Shoreline Drive would be worse, and planned to avoid it if at all possible.

She tried to think about the situation rationally, but her instinct said, go to the police. If Joel was not at the hotel, and nobody knew of his whereabouts, she decided she would file a report.

CHAPTER 33

(Present)

TJ opened his bedroom door and didn't hear any of the usual sounds within his house. It was uncommon not to hear garbled voices from the living room television. It was his dad's routine to fall asleep in his recliner with the TV turned up, causing commercials to play irritatingly loud.

TJ made his way to the top of the stairs and couldn't see any lights coming from the main level. Using the railing, he navigated down the stairs. In the living room, the curtains were still open, and weak light from the corner street lamp seeped into the room. It did not appear his parents were home, and without the noise from the television, the place was eerily quiet.

TJ went into the kitchen and picked up a note from the center island. Holding it at an angle near a window, he read, "Timmy, we received a call from the nursing home and needed to go in. There are left-overs in the fridge for you and your brother. See you soon. Love, Mom."

It was a strange time for his parents to be at the nursing home; he couldn't remember the last time they had visited. He knew it was a struggle for his mom; she had talked about the awkwardness of sitting in a room with a person who is unaware of who you are or why you are there.

TJ realized a perfect opportunity had presented itself, with his parents at the nursing home, and his brother not due back until late, he could revisit the lake. It was like circumstances had intervened on his behalf.

He had seen something in the woman's expression; he could not shake from his memory. And it was that vision, which haunted his dreams each night. She appeared to be asking for help, a plea that he tried to ignore, but the images were relentless, and he was desperate to restore normalcy to his life.

He didn't know anything about the woman, and his dreams were not logical, but logic was irrelevant. His nightmares were constant, and fear controlled his life. He had to break free from whatever force was holding him in its grips.

CHAPTER 34

(Present)

Mr. and Mrs. Schaffer had not been to see Mr. Williams in months. They did not see the point with his condition so deteriorated. Dementia had taken away the majority of his brain, and along with it, his ability to recognize his own family. When awake, Williams stared into space, and if he did happen to notice them, he would look confused or scared that people were in his room. Even though the Schaffer's had an understanding of the disease, they still felt his inability to recognize them, was somehow a failure on his part.

Arriving at the facility, a security guard ushered them into a small office near the nursing station. A few minutes later, the on-duty nurse came in to tell them Mr. Williams had passed earlier in the evening. Mrs. Schaffer, his daughter, was more relieved than anything else. They were not close, and she didn't have cherished memories from a father/daughter relationship.

The nurse went on to explain his death in clinical terms, concluding with a statement about his death being inevitable based on his multiple chronic illnesses. It all seemed a bit rehearsed like she was following a scripted procedure she had performed dozens of times in the past. She said the coroner had been notified and would give the official pronouncement of death.

CHAPTER 35
(Present)

Sam breathed a sigh of relief when she pulled under the portico of the Seven Lakes Grand Hotel. The blowing snow moving up Main Street, did so with the ferocity of a speeding train, with each gust more potent than the last. People with common sense, we're already hunkered down indoors, which included the hotel's valet service since no one appeared to offer to park her car. Leaving the engine running, she hurried inside the lobby — a valet who was chatting with a woman guest, saw Sam enter the lobby, and he hurried in her direction.

"Can I help you?" the college-aged looking young man called out.

"I am not a guest here." Sam responded as he came closer. "a good friend of mine is staying here. I don't know the room number." The young man giving Sam the once over tried to decide if she was legitimate.

"We're not allowed to give out room numbers, do you have any way to contact him?"

Sam guessed in his assessment; he assigned her the girlfriend role since she had not stated her good friend was a male.

"I have his cell phone number, I have tried to reach him all day, and he hasn't returned any of my calls." Listening to herself, she sounded like the crazy girlfriend and hoped the valet had not already put her in that category. Sam pressed on, "I need to know if you may have seen him or might know where he is. He drives a red 59 Bel Air; his name is Joel Vick." The mention of the car finally getting a positive reaction from the valet, and an immediate elevation of status to Sam for knowing Joel.

"Oh yeah, Joel, the detective, I brought his car around this morning, I don't think he has returned. Let me check the board." The young man disappearing into a small room to the side of the main entrance returned a few seconds later.

"No, he is still out, he left this morning around 10:00." Fear and anxiety rushed in, and Sam could feel a tightness in her chest. She made an effort not to show concern in front of the young man.

"Any idea of where he might have gone?" she asked calmly.

"No idea, he didn't say."

Sam nodded, "Listen, I appreciate your help. Can you tell him to call me if he returns?"

"Sure, no problem; what's your name?"

"Sam." She said as she turned toward the door, and pushing it open, walked out into the storm. Sitting inside her car, she was irritated at Joel's lack of communication, but her emotion was a cover for her real fear that he was in trouble.

CHAPTER 36

(Present)

Joel lost track of time inside the icehouse, he knew he had been there a long time, and was angry for getting into what he considered an avoidable situation. He had been trying the whole time to find a way out, but so far his attempts had been met with failure.

As he carefully climbed the cobblestone wall, he used the same footholds he had mentally mapped from his previous attempts. The last part of the climbing sequence was the hardest, where he tried to stand on the narrow ledge without the benefit of something to hold him against the wall. He had almost grasped something hard on his last attempt, but his balance failed, and he was unable to hold on.

With one knee throbbing, he had to use his weaker leg for the final push to the ledge. He used a back and forth motion similar to rocking a car stuck in the snow, to gain momentum before hoisting himself into a standing position on the ledge. With one last backward motion, he thrust his weight upward and used every ounce of energy to get into an upright position.

He experienced a couple of seconds of panic as his left hand swiped over the area without finding the attached object that he knew was there. Going up on his toes, he swiped his hand a third time, and this time grabbed hold of a u-shaped metal bracket. He was now securely on the ledge with a handhold to keep his balance. Standing there, he waited to recover his strength, exhausted from his repeated attempts.

Switching the hold to his right hand, he shimmied on the ledge to the left, to center himself under the bracket. Using his foot, he checked the space below the bracket and was thankful to find one in vertical alignment with the first. He suspected ramps used for loading the ice, would have attached to the brackets at different levels when filling the ice house. If true, he would have what amounted to a ladder to the top.

Testing his theory, he placed the foot from his right leg on the bracket below and pulled himself up using the handhold. Switching hands again, he swiped the area above and discovered another bracket in-line with the first two. Climbing up several more levels, he obtained a height that if he were to fall, it would be life-threatening.

The boards he had seen daylight through earlier from the floor were now within his reach, and ascending two additional brackets brought him to eye level with the openings. Looking outside, he was startled by the transformation that had taken place since his incarceration. A heavy snowfall had dramatically changed the landscape, and the snow continued falling at an astonishing rate.

Holding tight to the bracket with his left hand, he balled his right into a fist and, with a hammer-like motion, hit one of the cracked boards. The board moved out slightly, and with two additional hits, came loose from the building. Joel pushed it outward as far as he could reach, and the board cracked in half, tumbling into the snow below.

He climbed higher to use the strength of his leg, and, quickly dropped two more boards to the snow-covered ground. With the opening now large enough, he scrambled through to the exterior wall where a set of wooden cleats allowed him to navigate back to the ground. Slipping back under the fence near the trail, he was unaware his cell phone was lying just under the snow.

CHAPTER 37

(Present)

TJ dressed in layers, making sure to leave his water-proof ski-bib and jacket for last. The coat, a bright yellow, looked like something rescue workers would wear in inclement weather. The winter clothes were a gift from his parents the previous Christmas and already showed signs of being outgrown.

Leaving out the front door, he half hoped to see his brother coming up the drive, home early from his game. Cutting in front of the garage, he spotted the family's snow shovel, the full pan, designed for maximum snow removal. Picking it up, he rested its handle on his shoulder, the shovel in the air, looked like it was trying to catch the falling snow before it ever reached the ground. Walking down his driveway, he turned left onto the deserted residential street toward the lake. He had a feeling of empowerment from his new resolve as he set off for his destination.

Turning left a block before reaching Shoreline Drive; he planned to parallel the lake until he entered the woods where the city had converted an abandoned spur line into a walking path. The route would keep him protected from the wind until reaching the area he believed to be in-line with their previous nighttime excursion onto the ice.

After walking the first few blocks, he found it easier to drag the shovel behind him rather than carry it; the flat plane left a slight impression in the snow with a slightly deeper groove in the middle where the wooden handle attached.

When the spur path approached the warehouse district, TJ turned right toward the lake, cutting a trail through the wooded lot. Stepping from the edge of the woods, and starting across Shoreline Drive, he was surprised to see headlights coming toward him, the lights piercing the veil of falling snow, their distance hard to judge. He didn't hear the car's motor, but the lights seemed close. He only saw the lights for a couple of seconds before they abruptly veered toward the woods and disappeared altogether. He couldn't hear anything above the rushing wind that penetrated his layers of clothing and stung the exposed skin on his face.

Reaching the incline leading to the lake, he looked back in the direction of the headlights, and not seeing anything, slid down the slope to the edge of the lake. White-out conditions were prevalent just a dozen yards or so from the shoreline, and despite the danger, He continued with his mission, an invisible force pushing him forward.

Looking back at the path he had made through the snow gave him misguided comfort that he could retrace his steps if he got into a jam.

CHAPTER 38

(Present)

Joel nursing a bruised knee slid behind the wheel and started the Bel Air's engine. Getting back out, he pushed as much snow as he could with his hands and arms from the car's broad trunk before opening it to retrieve his ice scraper. Using the end with the brush, he cleared snow from the hood and windshield, and after several minutes of the engine running, the heat had sufficiently warmed the car hood to where he could slide the ice and snow to the ground.

Getting back in, he tossed the scraper into the backseat, and putting the car into gear, exited the parking lot. Turning left out of the lot, he headed back toward the lakeshore. Using slow, steady acceleration, he tried to avoid spinning the wheels on the snow-covered roadway. As he entered the turn, which brought Shoreline Drive back in parallel with the lakeshore, he let off the accelerator, carefully guiding the car through the bend. Joel, keeping his speed below the posted 35 mph speed limit, stared into the relentlessly falling snow, and estimated his visibility only 10 to 12 feet.

As he scanned the snow-covered roadbed ahead, a flash of yellow directly in his path caused him to hit his brakes hard. The Bel Air's nose veered right, while the back end swung around so that the car was sliding sideways in the roadbed. He felt the front left tire jump a curb and heard loud scraping noises as dense brush scraped across the hood before the car came to rest, its nose buried into the wooded lot.

"Holy shit," said Joel under his breath, still holding tight to the steering wheel. He was pretty sure the yellow he had seen was a person crossing Shoreline Drive.

With the Bel Air still running, he moved the shifter into reverse, and exerting light pressure on the gas pedal, attempted to back off the curb. His back tires spun and were unable to gain any traction to pull the heavy front end from its resting place at the edge of the woods. Shutting off the engine, he got out and walked in the direction of where he had seen the flash of yellow. About 10 feet from his car, he found footprints crossing the road and disappearing down the hill toward the lake. Looking down the incline, he could only see the tracks as far as the shoreline because of the blowing snow.

"Who in the hell ventures out in these conditions?" He asked himself. Joel knew he didn't have a choice; he needed to follow whoever it was onto the ice; the person could be in a life-threatening situation if they were to get lost.

CHAPTER 39

(Present)

Sam sitting in her car under the hotel's portico, waited another ten minutes, trying to figure a way she could avoid going to the police; she hated the bureaucracy, and she had no doubt it would be a condescending experience. She could not just sit idle, though; she had to do something; each moment that passed added to her anxiety

Googling the Seven Lakes Police, maps, indicated it was two minutes from her location. "Joel better be in trouble," she said to herself, as she put the car in gear and drove from the covered drive into what looked like an eight-inch accumulation of snow.

It was close to 7:00 PM when she arrived at the station. The doors were locked, and there was an old metal intercom box attached to the wall on the left side of the door. She mashed the single button, not feeling confident there was any connection to the device. After a few seconds, the box came to life with static, then a voice from the tiny speaker sounding small and distant said, "Can I help you?" It was hard to hear inflection with the low quality of sound, but the enthusiasm level felt similar to a fast-food encounter.

"Yes," Sam said, "I need to report a missing person." Sam cringed as soon as she said the words, imagining the person rolling their eyes, and waving other officers over to hear what was bound to be a good story.

The box crackled again with more static, and this time, she heard, "Ok, hold on." Another minute passed before she saw the light from a door opening in the dark hallway. An imposing uniformed female officer who walked to the exterior door where Sam stood looked her over before releasing the deadbolt to let her in.

CHAPTER 40

(Present)

Joel looking down at the footprints, noticed the person was pulling or dragging something flat that had little weight, judging from the weak depression it left in the snow. The impression and footprints were quickly losing definition from the volume of new snow falling. Joel walked back across the road toward the woods and saw that the person had come through the wooded lot before crossing Shoreline Drive and going down the embankment.

It was not a choice for Joel; he had to follow whoever it was; a person could swiftly perish in these conditions if lost. The fact that he didn't have his cell phone, made the situation that much more critical for both of them. There was no time to go for help and return, and the chances of somebody driving by in the next few minutes were remote.

Returning to his car, he opened the passenger door and flipping down the glove compartment, grabbed his revolver and LED flashlight. Slamming the door, he hurried back to the ridge and followed the tracks to the shoreline. He was surprised how deep the snow had become at the bottom of the incline, where he was still several yards from the actual ice. He sank into snow above his knees, before reaching the ice. Following the tracks on the ice, he was never able to see more than five to ten feet ahead at any given time. Every few minutes, he stopped to listen but only heard the rushing wind and drifting snow. The tiny ice crystals carried on the wind pelted his face, reminding him of sand kicked up in a summer storm.

It was hard to gauge distance, and he had forgotten to look at his watch when starting, so even rudimentary calculations were lost to him. Joel believed the tracks he followed so far, had been running in a straight line but knew that impression could be deceiving.

Conscious of the fact that if the person he followed stopped, Joel would almost certainly come upon him with little warning. Depending on the person, and their purpose, the meeting at least had the potential to turn bad. To reduce his risk of a surprise encounter, he continued to stop every few minutes and listen for any activity ahead.

CHAPTER 41

(Present)

TJ kept a steady forward momentum as he broke a path through the newly fallen snow across the ice. He was not good at making decisions and usually chose inaction when afraid of the unknown. Tonight was a different story; tonight, fear and determination were the drivers controlling his actions.

The woman's face in the ice had scared him badly, and he hadn't had a good night's sleep since. The idea of finding the same spot on the ice, with nothing to guide him in the middle of a snowstorm, was not a concern. Whatever was pushing him, he believed, would also guide him.

The shoreline or anything else familiar, was no longer visible. TJ was alone in the storm, and at times, if the wind died down, almost felt a sense of calm. These moments were fleeting and reminded him of a story he read in a science magazine about the eye of a hurricane.

His internal voice told him not to be afraid; that everything would be ok. He struggled to contain his fear of being lost, of the woman, of the storm. He needed to keep it together, if he let fear get the best of him, it would lead to indecision, and lock him in place. Every time fear bubbled up; he redoubled his efforts to tamp it down.

The wind having let up momentarily caused the blowing snow to thin, and TJ could scarcely believe the horror that now confronted him. A woman dressed in black, not ten feet from him, stood motionless, facing his direction. Thoughts moved at incredible speed; as he tried to reason how another person could be in this remote location, and each idea immediately rejected.

"How is it possible someone is here?"

"It's not,"

"Is she real?"

"Could it be an illusion?"

"Does she see me?"

TJ could not take his eyes from the figure who only had dark shadows where her features should have been. A large gust violently buffeted him from the side and moved a curtain of snow between him and the horrifying scene. When the wind died down, and visibility returned, she was no longer there.

Initially relieved, a new terrifying thought occurred to him. What if the woman had used the blinding snow to move closer to him? She could be behind him now, waiting to reach out for him. Every flight signal in his body screamed of the danger of his predicament. His heart pounded in his chest, and the vibration spreading through his limbs, caused his whole body to tremble. He could not move from the spot and had effectively been frozen in place by fear.

A pressure clamped his right shoulder from behind, and instinctively jerking his head in the direction of the force; he saw a gloved hand on his jacket. TJ pitched forward, like being shot from a cannon. The momentum forcibly removing the gloved hand from his shoulder, and at the same time, losing his balance, fell forward. TJ flailed wildly with his hands and feet trying to crawl forward by pushing frantically with his boots and knees to separate him as far as possible from whatever or whoever had grabbed him.

Somewhere amid his panic, he heard a voice, "I am sorry, I didn't mean to scare you, I'm not going to hurt you, I'm not going to hurt you."

In his panicked state, unable to process the words, a few of them still made it through. The voice was male, and the words spoken in a calming manner.

"I am trying to help you."

"Are you ok?"

" What are you doing out here?"

"My name is Joel; I am a detective."

TJ, finally realizing it was not the woman who had been standing in the distance, stopped flailing about, and cautiously turned back to look in the direction of the voice. He saw a tall man, holding his hands out with his palms open.

CHAPTER 42

(Present)

The officer led Sam down the dark hallway and into an inner office area, which had a dispatch and several desks set up for officers to fill out their reports. The room, harshly lit with fluorescent lights, was mostly empty except for the officer she followed, and one other female officer working dispatch within a small glassed-in room with its lights turned low.

The officer motioned Sam toward a small desk and then continued toward the back of the room where she retrieved paperwork from a filing cabinet. Returning, she sat opposite Sam.

"My name is Officer Ramirez, and I will be taking your statement." She said in a matter of fact tone. Ramirez spread several sheets of paper across the desk, and looking up at Sam, she asked her for her full name. Before Sam could respond, a male voice came across the dispatch radio.

Sam guessed the glass enclosure was meant as a separator because it certainly wasn't soundproof. She could hear every word coming across the radio. It took her a few seconds to understand the person talking, drove one of the town's snowplows. The driver's report was about an abandoned car on Shoreline drive. He told the dispatch operator that the vehicle had slid partially into a wooded lot. Sam's ears perked up when the driver described the car as a classic from the 50s or 60s.

Sam saw the impatient expression on Ramirez's face and quickly explained that the person she was here to report missing, drove an old Bel Air. Sam asked her if the dispatcher could get an ID on the make from the driver? Ramirez, eager not to have to fill out the paperwork, walked to the window and tapping lightly, asked her to get the model from the driver. A couple of minutes later, Sam heard the driver say Bel Air.

CHAPTER 43

(Present)

It had only been a few seconds after Joel stopped to listen, that he heard what sounded like a gasp from ahead — moving forward cautiously, the silhouette of a young person appeared, framed against the backdrop of the rapidly falling snow. The person stood still, looking straight ahead as though frozen in place, the storm moving in every direction around him. The person's height and stature was that of a kid and confirmed he had made the right decision to follow the person onto the ice. He spotted an aluminum shovel, the source of the impression he had noticed near the road. The handle clutched in the young person's gloved hand.

"What is he doing?" Joel asked himself, as he inched forward until within a few feet. Joel could now see it was a young boy, probably in his early teens. Not wanting to startle him by calling out, Joel moved closer until he was able to place his hand on the boy's shoulder. Joel, unprepared for his reaction, his hand flung off as the boy violently pitched forward and falling in an attempt to escape. Sprawled in the snow, he flailed his arms and legs, trying to move away from Joel. Startled by the boy's reaction, he initially could only watch as the boy pushed himself across the snow and ice on his stomach.

Joel calls out, trying to convince him he is here to help. Not making any moves in the boy's direction, Joel, communicates in a calm, steady tone. The boy, still trying to pull away, loses some urgency in his efforts, and after another minute, stops struggling altogether. Finally, turning back to look at Joel. "everything is going to be ok," Joel said when seeing the look of fear on the young boy's face.

When the boy stood up, Joel saw he was even younger than he had realized. He acted disoriented and nervously kept looking in the direction he had been facing. Joel looking down at the shovel the boy had left behind in his struggle to escape, asked, "What are you doing out here with a shovel?" The boy seemed surprised at seeing the shovel lying flat in the snow like he was seeing it for the first time.

Looking from the shovel to Joel, he said something that sent a chill through Joel that had nothing to do with the cold. "I have bad dreams," he said to no one in particular. The statement hung in the air like an odd proclamation amid the storm, and for Joel, no other explanation was necessary. Studying the boy's face, he considered the torment that had driven him to this extreme.

"Have you seen her tonight?" Joel asked. The boy held Joel's gaze for a few seconds before looking at the ground and nodding yes.

"Is that why you stopped?" the boy nodded again.

"Where did you see her?" The boy turned in the direction he had been facing and pointed into the cascade of falling snow.

Still facing away, he said, "She looked at me, but didn't have eyes." His voice, a monotone narration, described the scene that had stopped him cold. Joel walking past him in the direction he faced, made sure to keep several feet between them, so as not to startle him again. On the surface, there was an expanse of approximately five feet of unbroken snow, before an area of disturbance. The disturbed area had nothing to or away from it. She was real enough to leave an impression Joel thought to himself.

Turning to the boy, Joel asked, "You are the young man from the newspaper who saw the face in the ice?" TJ nodded again, this time keeping his eyes on Joel.

"What were you planning to do with the shovel? Joel asked.

"I don't know; I thought I could help," TJ said.

"I saw her"

Joel nodded, "I know, it is going to be ok. Do you think this is the spot where you saw her that night?

"She needed help." TJ continued, as if not hearing Joel's question. "Her lips moved, she was saying, HELP ME," Another shiver ran through Joel as he pictured the scene.

Joel moved closer to the boy to look into his eyes; he seemed in a trance from shock.

"I think she is here, Joel pointed toward the ice. I think she is on the bottom of the lake here." This information coming from an adult got through to TJ, and he looked up with a questioning expression.

"I believe she died a long time ago, and her body was put here in the lake at this spot. Ninety years ago, a young woman disappeared in a snowstorm, a storm much like tonight, and never seen again. She left the Seven Lakes Hotel in the middle of a storm. I believe she became a victim, got entangled with some bad people, ended up dead. Whoever did it, placed her in the lake to cover up the crime." Joel paused, "Your Grandfather knew something about what happened; he would have been about your age at the time. He wrote me a letter, said he had seen something the night she went missing." TJ's eyes got wider when hearing about a connection to his Grandfather.

Joel continued, "I think we will find if we examine this section of the lake" Joel swept his arm, indicating, the area around them, "that the initial channel they opened long ago to harvest ice, will line up with this spot." TJ had seen pictures of the ice harvesting operation in history class at school, black and white photographs of men standing near open water with poles guiding floating blocks of ice.

Joel picking up the shovel, placed the pan into the snow so that the handle stuck straight up.

"We need a police diver to explore the lake bottom here." Said Joel. TJ's face brightened a bit with the mention of the police. Things were no-longer spinning out of control, somebody had taken charge, maybe matters can get set right, and his nightmares might come to an end.

Joel could hear the unmistakable sound of snowmobile engines in the distance. He could tell they were running at a low RPM, probably following their tracks after discovering his abandoned car.

CHAPTER 44
(Present)

It seems as if there are only two colors left in the exterior world after a snowstorm, White and a blue so deep, one could easily imagine falling into its depths.

Joel quietly slid from between the sheets and looked back at Sam, who is sleeping soundly on her stomach. Her black hair let down, partially covered the side of her face, and draped across her bare shoulders and back. He would never forget the look of relief on her face when he arrived at the police station with TJ. He couldn't remember another time when someone had showed such concern for his well-being.

Padding across the carpet to the balcony doors, he looked out upon a magnificent panorama of white, capped with a deep blue sky. Just visible about a mile to the left of the hotel, a bright orange tent on the ice, looked tiny from this distance. A State Police dive team called in to explore the lake bottom in and around the area marked by TJ's shovel. He felt pretty confident the team would find Mary's remains on the lake bottom.

He heard a soft vibration from his phone lying face down on the carpet near the bed. Picking it up, he saw the caller had a local area code. Not wanting to disturb Sam, he let it go to voice mail while hurriedly putting on a pair of jeans and a t-shirt. Stepping into the hallway, he quietly closed the room door and went down to the lobby coffee shop to call the number back.

The person on the other end said, “Detective Sims, may I help you?” Joel had not talked to Sims since the day he had visited the police department and was surprised to hear from him now.

“Hey Sims, this is Joel, from Minneapolis,”

“Oh yeah, I called you a few minutes ago, I have an update on the incident in your hotel room.” Joel had not reported the incident but was pretty sure he knew a suspect who had.

“Great, what did you find out?”

“We have a clear picture of a license plate from an exterior camera on one of the retail spaces attached to the hotel. The person who belongs to the car also shows up on lobby cameras coming and going in a timeframe consistent with the incident.”

“Do you know who it is?”

“Yeah, we ran the plates, his name is Brad Tompkins, lives in Fairview.”

“We notified the Fairview police, do you plan to press charges?”

“I doubt it, but I am interested in his motive.”

“We’ll have the Fairview police pick him up for questioning.”

“Thanks, Sims, I appreciate the quick work.”

“I understand you are causing quite a stir with the Mary Benton case,” Sims said, “I saw the State Police and their crime lab boys coming in this morning.”

“I have my fingers crossed that we might learn enough to piece her story together.” Replied Joel.

“Alright, let me know if I can help,” said Sims before ending the call.

Joel ordered a latte for himself, and a straight black coffee for Sam before returning to the room.

When entering, he heard the shower running and waited in the main room for Sam to finish. Coming out of the bathroom, Sam had wrapped herself in one of the terry cloth robes provided by the hotel. Seeing Joel, she hurried over and kissed him on the lips before stepping back with a broad smile.

"I thought you had already left me," She said, still smiling.

"No, nothing quite so dramatic, I received a call from the local police, you were still sleeping, so I went to the coffee shop to see if it was important."

"Was it?"

"It was detective Sims, the guy who the chief assigned to help me with the department. He said they found the person suspected of breaking into my room. I don't even understand how the police knew about that." Joel said, looking at Sam with a questioning expression.

Sam, looking sheepish, said, "lucky guess?"

"So, who was he?" She asked.

"Somebody from your neck of the woods lives in Fairview."

"Really?"

"Yeah, a guy by the name of "Brad Tompkins."

"Oh my God, you're kidding me?"

"What, you know him?"

"I am so sorry."

Joel could see she was genuinely upset.

"Sam, who is he?"

"This is so embarrassing." She said, turning away from Joel.

"I dated him about six months ago; we only went out a couple of times; he was a total control freak; I ended it abruptly. He left me some not so friendly messages, but that was about it."

"Sam, it is not your fault, the guy has a problem."

"God, I hate that I put you in danger,"

"You didn't; you had nothing to do with what he did."

Walking back to Joel who sat on the edge of the bed, she stood in front of him and put her hands on his shoulders, "I would never have been able to live with myself if something had happened to you."

Leaning in, she kissed him softly on the lips.

Joel untied her robe and slipping it off her shoulders; let it drop to the floor.

CHAPTER 45

(Present)

Joel sitting in the lounge of the hotel's lobby, watched the weather channel track the storm that had dumped 15 inches of snow on Seven Lakes. The storm moving in a southeasterly direction delivered a glancing blow to the Twin Cities before setting its sights on Wisconsin and Chicago beyond.

Sam had left a little before noon when the highway to Fairview was reported clear. She planned to work a half-day at the museum on a project with a looming deadline. Joel, accompanying her to the lobby, felt awkward saying goodbye without knowing when he might see her again.

He hated waiting around the hotel and the fact that he had no conduit for information from the State Police, or for that matter, the Seven Lakes Police. He didn't have a "Marty," here, and he was growing impatient for news from the dive. He thought about calling Sims, but for reasons, he couldn't explain, decided against it.

Walking to one of the towering windows facing the lake, he tried to see the orange tent that had been visible from his room, but the marina building near the shore blocked his view in that direction.

Joel's phone still set to silent vibrated in his pocket; the frequency of the vibrations always seeming to have more urgency than its audio equivalent.

"Joel Vick." He said, answering the call.

"Joel, this is Chief Swanson, there's a Captain Sterns with the State Police requesting a meeting with you. Are you available at 3:00? No reason for the Chief to engage in small talk, Joel thought.

"Absolutely," he replied, "Do you know if their divers found anything?"

" I am pretty sure that is why he wants to talk with you,"

"I'll be there," and without further acknowledgment, Swanson ended the call.

Arriving early, Joel opened the door into the large room where he had first met Sims and the Chief. Today the room was more active, with several desks occupied by both uniformed and plain-clothes officers. Joel told a uniformed officer he was here to see Capt Sterns. The officer nodded and told him to take a seat; Sterns will be right back.

A few minutes later, the hallway door opened, and a man in jeans and a long-sleeve button-down plaid shirt with running shoes entered the reception area. He looked to be in his early thirties, with close-cut hair, a chiseled face and a manner suggestive of a military background. The man spotting Joel, asked, "You Joel Vick?"

"Yes, you must be Captain Sterns."

"Too formal," he said, "call me John. The Chief told me we could use his office; I believe he has left for the day." Joel followed Sterns into the office with the uncomfortable straight back chairs he remembered from his first visit. Once settled, Sterns asked Joel about his investigation of Mary, and as Joel talked, Sterns took meticulous notes.

"What I am curious about," Sterns said after several minutes, "is how in the hell you could pinpoint the location of a body under the ice?"

For Joel, the long answer was more complex and delved into gray areas on the fringes of the paranormal. Williams, alluding to a restless soul in his letter, and TJ, his Grandson, in a nearly trance-like state on the ice. Joel believed there was a connection between the two, triggered by Williams's death that same evening. For Sterns, though, Joel decided he would stick to more conventional facts. "I built my theories based on circumstantial evidence. I was able with high confidence, to put Mary and Patterson at a Christmas celebration the night before she vanished. Patterson was a person of interest from the beginning. He was the person in a photograph Williams had on his nightstand at the nursing home; he had involvement with the Seven Lakes Ice Works as a representative of the railroad; he had an office in their administration building." Joel paused, "It always bothered me that Mary's body never turned up. While researching, I stumbled across what I believed to be the answer."

"What did you find?"

"An article published after the 1925 storm that talked about the difficulty of removing the snow from the ice field before the harvest could resume. It mentioned the workers on the first day of operations, before the storm hit, opening a channel used to float ice blocks to the conveyor." Joel looked up at Sterns to see if he was following. Sterns understood what he was getting at, "the open ice, created a perfect place to stash a body." Sterns said, completing the thought.

"It was the only plausible solution I could come up with for the missing body," Joel replied. Sterns said: "You have another problem, based on what you have told me about Mary, the skeletal remains are not hers."

Joel, stunned, felt like he had been gut-punched. "What do you mean?"

"I mean, the remains we found are from someone much older, probably closer to 60."

"Oh my God, his wife," Joel exclaimed.

"Whose wife?" asked Sterns.

" I completely missed it," Joel said, ignoring the question.

"What did you miss?"

"Lucy Patterson, Charles Patterson's wife," Joel said, shaking his head in disbelief."What was the scene like on the lake bottom? Joel asked.

"Like foul play." Replied Sterns. "She was attached to a metal sled with cable; there was a long pole that looked to be one of the tools used in the ice harvesting operation lashed to the sled. The examiner thought it possible the pole, with its sharp end, could be the instrument that killed her. The cable was wrapped multiple times around the sled. We think when pushed into the water, the whole contraption turned upside down on the way to the bottom. In effect, it embedded her body in the muck with the sled on top of her. A lack of oxygen within the muck slowed the decomposition of her bones. They were in relatively good shape for their age."

"Any idea how she died?"

"Several of her right side ribs were broken. According to the examiner, the angle of the breaks would have been nearly impossible for someone to inflict. He said it was more likely she suffered an accident. The injuries were consistent with being impaled, the weight of her body against the sharp object doing the damage."

"The question then becomes, why cover it up? If death is an accident." Said, Sterns.

"Because Mary is there, it puts her and Patterson in a compromising position, with Patterson having everything to lose. Mary, a victim of circumstance, was likely desperate, and looking to Patterson, with God, knows what in mind. Patterson's wife suspecting something arrives on the scene and winds up dead. Mary, with knowledge of her death and disposal, becomes a person Patterson needs to keep quiet."

"What happens to Mary?"

"I don't know."

"So, what do you do now?"

Joel smiled, "I hadn't thought that far ahead."

"I appreciate the work you put in on this case, and your willingness to share it. Take my card and text. me your contact information, and I will notify our lab to copy you on anything else they might find." Joel stood and shook Sterns's hand before leaving the County building and walking back to the hotel.

While packing his clothes, he called down for the valet to bring his car around. Leaving from the Seven Lakes Grand driveway, he turned toward the shoreline and, taking a left at the light, drove until he saw the Tudor. Parking in the same spot as the day he arrived, Joel getting out of the car, could feel the icy grip that had been in place since his arrival easing back today, with the temperature soaring to a nearly balmy 30 degrees.

There was a small child in the front yard of the Tudor with a red plastic sled trying unsuccessfully to slide through the deep snow of the gently sloping yard. Looking at the house, he wondered if the person in the shadows of the photograph had been Mary. He thought about the recluse the reporter talked about, could that have been her?, had she lived out a secret life in Seven lakes?

Getting back into his car, he drove out of town toward the interchange that would lead him back to the cities. An hour later, he found himself standing on the threshold of the research room at the Fairview museum watching Sam bathed in light from her computer screen, her fingers lightly moving across the flat keyboard in front of her monitor. Sensing a presence, she turned and looked in his direction, and seeing Joel, leaped out of her seat, and running across the floor, launched herself into his arms.

"Joel, what are you doing here, I thought you were back in the cities by now; I was preparing myself for a lonely night of NetFlix and leftovers," Joel explained what he had learned from Sterns. Sam, with a faraway look, considered the implications of the new information.

"I don't want to think about what that might have meant for Mary." Sam finally said.

Joe nodded, "Patterson was a cruel character who probably dumped his wife into the frozen lake. Mary, scared to death and likely under his influence, would have been easy to manipulate. If those were the conditions, I don't like her odds."

"What are you going to do now?"

"She's still missing; it's still a cold case; we have to keep looking."

CHAPTER 46

(Present)

It was early evening before Joel left Fairview for the cities. It had been painful saying goodbye to Sam for the second time on the same day, and he was still feeling frustrated about not having solved the case. As Joel drove south from Fairview, the sun dropped below the horizon, and the sky transformed into a mosaic of purples in-between scattered cloud remnants.His route took him through snow-covered farmland, and he thought about unresolved details of the case, like the small piece of lace and what it might have meant to Williams.

His knee banged up from his multiple escape attempts from inside the Ice House, started to throb, and despite re-positioning his leg every few minutes, he was unable to find a spot offering any relief. He decided to stop in the next town and purchase a bag of ice to reduce the swelling. The small towns along the route had descriptive names, but all looked pretty much the same. A Liquor store, a Holiday gas station, and some type of lodging seemed to be prerequisites.

Parking at a gas pump and exiting the car, Joel performed a combination stretch and limping maneuver as he entered the store. When inside, he realized his awkward gait had garnered attention from a few of the patrons. Grabbing a package of his favorite coconut crunch mini donuts, he made his way to the coffee counter. The coffee pot on the burner looked like it had been there a while; the black liquid undoubtedly both bitter and potent. "Just what the doctor ordered," he thought before filling a large styrofoam cup.

Placing the items on the counter, he told the clerk he needed $30.00 on number three, and a bag of ice. The clerk, a tall skinny man with shoulder-length hair, held up his hands, saying, "It is the damndest thing, here we are in the middle of numb-nuts, Minnesota, and we are completely out of ice, pretty ironic, ha?" Joel nodded in agreement. "The box went on the fritz; boss said it was the compressor, hadn't ordered ice in days." Feeling some pressure to respond when the clerk paused and stared at Joel, he said, "It's OK, I'll stop in the next town."

"Sorry for the inconvenience, I guess everything breaks at some point, don't remember that box ever being empty before."

"Yea." Joel said, "You never know."

Joel, climbing inside the car after pumping gas, was about to turn the key in the ignition when he suddenly sat back in his seat and slapped his right leg. "Son of a bitch." He said out loud, "I know where she is." Pulling out his wallet, he looked through the business cards he kept in the paper money section, trying to find Sterns's card. Finding it, he punched in the number.

"Sterns," a voice said after the second ring.

"Hey Sterns, this is detective Joel Vick."

"Joel!, I didn't expect to hear from you so soon."

"I think I know where she is."

"Really, who?"

"Mary"

"Where?"

"The year Mary went missing was the first year anyone in Seven Lakes could remember the Ice Works, running out of locally stored ice."

"And?"

"I was locked in the old Ice House the day of the rescue on the lake… don't ask; it's a long story?"

"OK"

"The floor is several feet below grade with a cobblestone foundation. The floor is dirt, probably something to do with the weight of the ice or insulation, I don't know."

"Still not getting it."

"The company had been in operation for 50+ years by that point. Nobody could ever remember the storage facility running out of ice before that year."

"Got it, pretty safe place to stash a body under tons of ice."

"Exactly."

"We have one of those fancy "Ground Penetrating Radar" (GPR) units somewhere. I can get a crime lab crew in there to have a look. Text me the location and how we gain access."

"Will do."

"Normally, I would require a little more information than a hunch to commit resources, but I have the feeling your suspicions have underlying support. I don't want to know; I would just be happy to put one in the closed column."

"I think the young woman had a pretty tragic life, and I am guessing it ended abruptly and violently. I do appreciate your help with this." Joel said.

"Hey, it's what we do." Said Sterns before hanging up.

Upon returning to his apartment in Minneapolis, Joel fell asleep, the minute his head hit the pillow. Not realizing his level of exhaustion, he slept until nearly 11:00 AM. While waiting for a pot of coffee to brew in the unfamiliar kitchen, Joel looked around the apartment as if seeing it for the first time. Somehow the place seemed a bit homier than he remembered.

Pouring a cup of coffee and sitting at the café style breakfast nook, he pressed Sam's number on his phone and was pleased to hear her cheerful voice answering.

"So, you are calling to see if you can take me to lunch?" she teased.

"I wish,"

"I was hoping you would call."

"Well, its official business about the case."

"Oh, the honeymoon is already over; what's going on?"

Joel relayed what he had told Sterns, and how Sterns committed to putting a team with a GPR machine inside the old Ice House to see if they could find any anomalies below the dirt floor. Sam agreed it all made sense, and now wondered if there was something more to the story of Joel ending up locked inside. They talked about the case for another thirty minutes before Sam had to attend a previously scheduled appointment.

At 6:24 PM, Joel's phone started vibrating from on top of the kitchen counter. Joel saw it was Sterns's number before he answered.

"Joel Vick."

"Joel, it looks like you are two for two. I just talked to the team running the GPR tests, and they have a definite hit. The technician who has investigated a lot of crime scenes said he is 99% positive they will be excavating human remains with the readings he is seeing."

Joel had a feeling of both relief and sadness. A crime undoubtedly had occurred on that stormy night in 1925, and Williams likely witnessed some part of the series of events leading to Mary's death. The entry in the police report log of an unreliable witness combined with a nearly nonexistent investigation looked suspicious. In a perfect world, justice would be incorruptible. Unfortunately, people with money and power are often exempt from an unbiased criminal justice system, and their heinous crimes sometimes go unanswered in this world.

Joel, thanking Sterns, knew the bones they would uncover in the Ice House would ultimately belong to Mary, and her missing person file could finally close. Joel, feeling optimistic about his future, thought about the unfairness of circumstance and how finding Mary was such a small consolation compared to the injustice she must have endured.